Center for Basque Studies
Basque Literature Series, No. 4

BASQUE LITERATURE SERIES

ANJEL LERTXUNDI

Perfect Happiness

Translated from Basque by
Amaia Gabantxo

Basque Literature Series Editor
Mari Jose Olaziregi

Center for Basque Studies
University of Nevada, Reno

Center for Basque Studies
Basque Literature Series, No. 4

Center for Basque Studies
University of Nevada, Reno
Reno, Nevada 89557
http://basque.unr.edu

Series design © 2007 by Jose Luis Agote.
Cover painting by Jose Luis Zumeta.

          Library of Congress Cataloging-in-Publication Data

Lertxundi, Anjel.
  [Zorion perfektua. English]
  Perfect happiness / Anjel Lertxundi ; translated from Basque by
Amaia Gabantxo.
      p. cm. -- (Basque literature series ; no. 4)
  Summary: "A realist novel that explores the effect that witnessing a
terrorist assassination has on a sixteen-year-old girl's life"--Provided
by publisher.
  ISBN 978-1-877802-74-4 (pbk.)
  I. Gabantxo, Amaia. II. Title. III. Series.

  PH5339.L4Z6713 2007
  899.92--dc22

                                          2007010370

The Center for Basque Studies wishes to gratefully acknowledge the generous financial support of the Government of the Basque Autonomous Community for the publication of this book.

ANJEL LERTXUNDI

Perfect Happiness

I believe we must awaken the conscience of memory.

CARMEN BAROJA NESSI

Without conscience we would be animals,
close to a state of perfect happiness.

PERTI

1

I closed the door and turned the light on. Even then, the staircase and hallway were in semi-darkness, because the dim lonesome bulb provided only a pitiful light, as always. There was a stale smell in the air, as always. I held the flap of my bag under my chin and put the scores in. I ran down the stairs, wanting to get away as quickly as possible. I needed to leave the scales and the arpeggios, the fingering, the piano teacher and the music academy behind.

The moment I stepped outside, a sharp, cold wind hit me in the face. I felt better. I turned up the lapels of my jacket and walked toward the beach instead of taking the path that led from the train station, as I did every evening. I could no longer hear the sounds of the piano. *Will I see him today?* I thought, my heart beating wildly, anticipating the possibility of bumping into the boy I liked. My happiness didn't last long. I remembered the threat my teacher had issued five minutes earlier:

"I won't be able to accept your application to take the exam at the conservatoire. Not until you've mastered *Bonheur parfait* completely."

I groaned. I would never be able to perfect the mechanics of the last section of Schumann's piece, where the two hands must play as if they are talking to each other.

"The right hand must allow the left to take precedence, *the left* is the protagonist, *the left* is the protagonist, *the left* is the protagonist . . ."

Even today that is precisely my downfall: the need to concentrate on the left means that the right hand ends up playing without vigor, out of sync, sounding clunky. It is the lack of balance between the two that is the problem. My left is weak, and I have had to make a deliberate effort to improve it practically since the day I started playing. Thanks to the time and dedication I have poured into correcting my flaw I have no trouble playing with my left hand alone. I can play extremely technical one-hand passages equally well with my left or right hand; no one would think I'm not left-handed. So the only difficulty I'm faced with is the intrinsic difficulty of the piece I choose to play. My trouble starts when the piece requires that the left take precedence and the right only accompany; on such occasions my right slackens and refuses to accompany the left. The right does not know how to be subservient to the left—that is the problem. It's quite common among right-handed pianists, but unfortunately that offers little consolation.

To this day I can hear my teacher's words, complete with the rhetorical flourishes that were so typical of her:

"When do they converge? Where do the incoming and outgoing tides meet? It can't be pinpointed, no one can say exactly when it happens, and yet this miracle has happened twice daily since the dawn of time. In the same way, one hand must allow the other to take over, exactly as the tides do. It can't be forced, it can't be detected, it must be done *con sottigliezza*, our ear must not be able to pick it up."

I love Schumann, his piano pieces in particular. I find them simple and natural: they aren't difficult to play, the keys respond to the touch of the fingers effortlessly. But paradoxically, Schumann's pieces are difficult precisely because they are simple: if the piano is played without *sottigliezza* the music loses all its charm; at best it sounds only half-way there, not melancholic enough. And Schumann without the melancholy isn't really Schumann.

I was stuck in that halfway place and could not submit to the melancholic trance some of Schumann's pieces demanded, especially *Bonheur parfait*. When I started playing, I was always conscious of the imminent change of tone, and as a result could never concentrate on the score. *Almost there! Now, right now!* And when I arrived at that complicated turning point, the change would be too sudden, too brusque. Or too fast. Obvious enough, in any case, to my teacher's ears—and mine, too.

My teacher would give me the same advice Schumann gave his lover Clara Wieck: "You'll enjoy these pieces more if you forget about technique."

Instead of helping me, those words made me more nervous.

It wasn't easy for me; my way of playing the piano is more technical than intuitive. I'm not a virtuoso.

I'd have to spend another year at the local high school. Worse, I'd have to keep going to the same music academy.

Another year of listening to my teacher's metaphors about tides.

Bonheur parfait! Perfect happiness, indeed.

The bells rang, dark and slow. One, two . . . up to eight. I looked at my watch. It was in time with the tolling of the bells. As usual in the evening, a man was closing the iron gates to stop the junkies from spending the night under the church's front awning.

I started to walk faster; I knew that telling my mother that the piano exercises had delayed me again would not appease her. She was obsessed with punctuality. Being on time was sacred. For my mother, life's inevitable unexpected events were mere excuses, unless irrefutable evidence was offered to the contrary.

The smell of rain clung to the falling dusk. Somber clouds filled the sky and the wind rushing from the alleys between houses sounded like angry wasps. I dug my head between my shoulders and tugged the lapels of my jacket closer to my cheeks.

From a small bar came the rasping voice of a well-known singer and the tic-tac-tac of a pinball machine.

I looked right and left to make sure none of my parents' acquaintances were around. Only a dark-haired man walked toward the bar. No one else. No risk. Sheltered under a balcony next to the bar, I lit a cigarette. I took the first drag avidly.

At that precise moment, a shadow dashes from the alley beside the bar. It approaches the dark-haired man. And then I hear: *Bang!* a tiny explosion, a dry sound, like the noise shutters make when the wind hurls them against the wall.

A scream drowns in the dark-haired man's throat, and he looks at me. My cigarette falls to the ground. His eyes seem about to explode, they shine like glass held against the light. He stares at me. He opens his mouth: the smile on his face is silly and anguished at the same time. I doubt he knows what's happening to him. Then he starts to fall, very, very slowly, as if he's asking a silent question. His knees crack, and to avoid hitting the ground, he grabs at the only hold within reach: a concrete flowerpot, white with seagull droppings.

There are bunches of violet flowers in the flowerpot. A subtle vanilla scent emanates from them. Blood flows from the corner of the man's mouth. The voice of the well-known singer and the pinball machine have suddenly gone quiet.

I hear steps moving quickly toward me. I imagine what's about to happen. I press my fists against my mouth and shut my eyes. *Bang!* I hear again. *Bang! Bang!* I don't move. I can't. Even when car tires screech behind me I remain frozen.

At some point I open my eyes.

The man stands perfectly still, his hands stretched toward the flowerpot.

A seagull's shadow, flying from the open sea to the enclosed streets. The bird circles twice, tentatively, looking for a place to alight. Its wings beat the air and it heads seaward again. The wind blows tumultuously through the alleys, whirling plastic bags, dry leaves, sand.

Suddenly, the dark-haired man's body makes a noise like a very heavy bag hitting the floor.

His mouth is open, probably more to allow his life to ebb away than to breathe. His eyes, however, are lost halfway between me and the flowerpot, and the two soft bags that underline them emphasize their darkness. He makes a small, futile movement, an attempt to lift his head off the ground. There's a strip of black leather around his neck, and, hanging from it, a *lauburu*, the Basque cross.

I shut my eyes again.

And I hear the man's head hit the ground.

It's over.

I remember not crying, being unable to find a lament within me. The dead man lay two meters from me. I was numb; I could only look at him. Some sort of emotion was lodged in my throat. It had traveled from the heart up. But I had no tears.

A tender, empty sentiment with no way of manifesting itself; that is the only way I can describe it.

My eyes followed the path of the blood flowing from the dead man's mouth: it ran from his face into the patterns on the flagstones toward my feet.

I took a step back.

The red rivulet flowed quickly and started to blend with the dust under the flowerpot.

A few young people came out of the small bar in complete silence; their shadows scurried away, shrinking against the wall. Maybe they wanted to become invisible.

I don't know how long I stood in front of the corpse, looking at the bloodstain forming on the pavement.

At one point, I realize I hear sirens approaching. They are only a noise, moving through the patterns of the streets, seeking a place to converge, like the blood on the pavement. One noise among many others. In no time, the sound, strong enough to silence the sea now, climbs over the curb and stops next to me. A second car arrives right away.

Three policemen step down from the first car, hands on their waists and eyes darting everywhere, assessing the risk. The ones in the second car place themselves strategically on street corners. When they think the situation is under control they signal to the first car and two more policemen step out. They walk out slowly looking right and left until they reach the dead man. Just as if someone had made a signal, as soon as the policemen arrive, people emerge from alleys and side streets, like cockroaches scuttling out of holes in an old, empty house. Fear is on their faces as they approach; they whisper to each other and try to remain hidden.

The police start shooing people away, shouting, "Step back! Step back!" Two of them examine the area around the body while the other two cordon it off with red and white tape.

The whispers start off low but grow and grow until they become a more effective wall of separation from the dead man than the tape itself. The tape distances me from him, but the onlookers' curiosity and babbling upset me.

I feel the urge to escape. I need to leave, run far away from here, hide in the black night like the blood hid under the flowerpot. I need to get into a cinema and listen to an hour and a half of *Bang! Bang!*, enough for a lifetime, and eat popcorn and drink Coke to my heart's content.

But my legs don't respond.

My head tells me to get out of there, to get out of there, but my legs can't obey the command; I have no strength, I can't move. The sound of more sirens fills the street. Nurses step out of ambulances, carrying bags of blood and stretchers. More police. "Step back! Everybody step back now!" A photographer comes closer; he's lanky and fashionably dressed and has a cigarette between his lips. He passes under the red and white tape and his camera flashes twice. He throws his cigarette away. The butt hits the ground, making little sparks. He steps on it.

No more sparks.

He looks at me with one eye half-closed, thinking something. He's gone. Suddenly I hear "Psst!" behind me.

I turn back, away from the dead man. He's there again, with his camera.

The flash blinds me.

He gives me a friendly wink. He turns and leaves as suddenly as he arrived.

2

I stayed there, rooted to the ground, paralyzed, staring at the body.

A doctor arrived. He kneeled down by the dead man and checked his pulse; put his ear to the man's chest; checked his pulse again. Then he stood up and signaled to the nurses to cover the body. Two who were standing by spread a sheet over the man.

Then I just looked at the sheet, so intently that after a while I realized I could see the contours of his face again, just as when we try to remember an old photograph we know is lost in some remote drawer—the salt-and-pepper hair; the small, sunken eyes with the two soft bags underneath them; the outline of his fine lips and the tobacco-stained, rust-colored teeth.

There was also his paleness, but I couldn't tell if this was a consequence of the shots or if his face was naturally waxen.

As for his age, I figured it was around the same as my father's. Maybe he was slightly younger. In any case, he was very lean and veiny: taut. Around forty-five years old, I decided, ascribing my father's age to the dead man.

All those characteristics, however, could just as well have belonged to a desiccated body. Both his profile and expression were frozen in time like those of a bronze statue. I couldn't complete the picture of his face because I couldn't infuse him with life or light up his eyes. The outline of the lips I was remembering was expressionless, and the blood that a few minutes ago had dribbled down the side of his mouth was now dry—on the ground as well as in my memory.

But I didn't have much time to reflect: more and more people were approaching and the low, gossipy murmur had become a loud prattle. They spoke without embarrassment, vociferously contributing their questions and hypotheses to the running conversation: the dead man was the bartender; he hadn't been living in town for long; he was a melancholy guy, quiet, seemed not to have any friends. *And to die like that, such a shame . . . he was always alone . . . and the coroner, where the hell is the coroner? . . . he never bothered anyone, but you never know . . .*

I saw a young couple holding hands come through the crowd, elbowing their way to the front. "Damn, we're too late! They've covered him up." The police, nurses, and photographers rushing back and forth, people's comments, the sound of sirens, the intermittent flashes . . . gradually it all began to look very much like the scenes I often saw on TV.

Suddenly, a nasal voice pierces the din behind me.

"What's this kid doing here?"

I turn around very slowly. Close by, a policeman stands staring at me. He seems to be in charge. People notice that I'm the kid he is referring to and take a step back to let him through. They all look at me. I see only their eyes. Vacant eyes, searching eyes, questioning eyes: *Yeah, exactly, what's the kid doing here? This isn't for her; she should be at home!*

Their eyes, however, show above all a burning curiosity; they look like eager players of some sort of game.

The policeman arrives at my side. He tilts his head back and looks at me differently from the other people.

His eyes are serious and high up, very high up. The wind blows the sparse hair of his receding hairline. But I'm not scared: the policeman is cross-eyed, like Perti, my chemistry teacher. Like Perti, he has to tilt his head back because that's the only way he can make both his eyes look in the same direction. So the policeman tilts his head back until his eyes meet my face.

But even then I wasn't scared. I was angry. Not because he had referred to me as a kid, or because I was put off by his strabismus—it was his tone, and the fact that he had questioned my right to be there. If anything I was more entitled than anyone to be there. It was true that I had never before seen the man who now lay on the ground, but as far as I was concerned, we were inextricably linked because I had seen him die: I was the only witness to the last spark of life in his eyes. To the cross-eyed policeman I was only a kid, but it was into my eyes and no one else's that the man had looked for the last time. My eyes, not the gunshot, were his last human experience. And that was why I was there: I was collecting the last moments of this man's life to keep in my memory.

Thanks to me, the man on the ground hadn't died looking into his killer's eyes.

But the policeman doesn't give a damn about my thoughts. There he stands, hands on hips, looking at me from the highest peak of his tilted head.

Another policeman comes over and whispers something in his ear. I take the opportunity to look at the dead man. I relax when I see the blanket-covered lump: he's still there.

When Grandpa died—I was seven—they didn't let me see his body, but I remember a dream I had around that time as clearly as if it had really happened. Grandpa was a broad-shouldered man; quiet, kind. In my dream, I saw him as he was, in the coffin, heedless of my parents' tears: "Are we not having dinner tonight, then?" he asks, as calm as anything. Then he lifts his head a bit and gives me a kiss. I get frightened and start to cry, and he tells me off playfully: "Silly monkey, don't you realize it's me, Grandpa?"

The thing was, I couldn't believe I'd never see him again. So I started to try to catch him unawares. I would suddenly go *peek-a-boo!* and look back, sure that I'd find him hiding behind me; or I would search for him from the doorway of the bar near the house. I used to think that he was looking for me, that was why I would go *peek-a-boo!* and check behind doors or inside wardrobes.

I was sure that they had forced him to disappear, to remain in hiding. Therefore, I concluded, death was to play hide and seek. When you leave a place, you know that the people and animals you've left behind are alive; you just don't see them. Death meant not seeing Grandpa, that was all.

The shrill, nasal voice of the policeman brought me back to reality.

"*¡Vete, haz el favor!*" he says in Spanish. He wants me to leave. His teeth are yellow. Uneven.

I try to find the right sort of excuse. I can think of a couple but they're too banal.

I turn my back to the policeman and head homeward quickly, zigzagging, as if I were walking down the aisle of a speeding train. I'm staring at the ground, unable to put what has happened in order. As though removing spider webs before my face, that's how I open pathways through my mangled thoughts.

Night is gathering at the rooftops. The wind smells of old paper, brings news of rain.

The elms on the beach front, the German hotel, the houses in front of the old sawmill. Fifteen minutes to get home. I'm later than I thought. I walk faster.

Suddenly, I see a boy walking toward me. *Not now!* I cringe with embarrassment; I don't know what to do. Who knows what I look like; he mustn't see me.

He had been in town for about six months. I had no idea where they had come from when I saw him and his family taking their furniture out of a moving van. Two other young guys also hung around the van. And a slim man I decided must be their father. But I chose my boy the moment I saw him. There was something in his eyes that broke down my defense mechanism. He was lanky, like a willow, and walked softly—but he seemed very sure of himself.

It starts to rain, calmly, softly. The boy takes out a small umbrella he's been holding under his arm.

I didn't know where he was from, I didn't know his name, all I knew was that he was studying journalism at the university. I started plotting ways of accidentally crossing his path since I first saw him by the moving van. I would wait for the bus to arrive. I would provoke unlikely coincidences in order to bump into him: "Is this bus going to San Sebastian?" The blood pounding in my brain, my heart about to explode, I would break into a sweat, embarrassed. When we met in the street we greeted each other. We never spoke. We would lift our heads a bit and smile childishly at each other, that was all.

That was all. My regret at not daring to do anything else filled the vacuum.

A fine drizzle, getting more persistent by the minute, becomes a heavy curtain of rain. The boy starts to walk faster.

The vacuum caused by the boy who was walking toward me with an open umbrella couldn't be more different from the empty feeling the dead man had left me with. The boy made me feel dizzy and at the same time instilled a bittersweet hope that the vacuum would one day disappear. The emptiness the dead man had left me with was very different, almost the opposite, in fact: a boundless void.

The boy is practically in front of me. The rain falls in thick drops now, without respite; it feels like the sky wants to empty itself.

Not now, please!

I put my bag on my head and pretend not to have seen the boy. I don't even look at him, even though I think he has lifted the umbrella and is about to say hello. I pretend not to recognize him.

Lightning illuminates the curtain of rain. I can feel the boy's steps softly splashing away from me. It seems he hasn't recognized me. I'm very relieved.

I regret not having worn my hooded jacket—the bag doesn't shelter me much. And there isn't much refuge under the roofs of the houses or the canopies of the chestnut trees. But even though I'm getting wet I'm starting to enjoy the rain, and I care less and less about not having worn my hooded jacket. I take the bag off my head and hang it from my shoulder. The rain falls freely down my face, my eyes, my cheeks, my mouth; my hands are free, and the rain drenches my hair, caresses my face and runs down my chest. I succumb to the sound of my footsteps on the wet pavement lit by streetlamps, on the puddles, on the patches of grass.

Then I remembered the blood. The rain would have erased it by now. But the dead man would be there, under the drenched sheet. I knew because I hadn't heard any sirens or seen any ambulances since the policeman forced me to leave.

My heart is dark; I run my tongue across my lips.

They taste salty and bitter.

3

When I get to my street I look up at our windows—someone seems to be standing behind the curtains. *Typical*, I think angrily, *Mom's waiting for me*. I climb the stairs trying to think of what to say to her. But I can't find the words.

Just as I'm about to put the key in the lock the door abruptly opens. I stand with my heart in my throat; my mother with anger in her eyes.

"Do you realize how late it is? And what's the excuse today?"

She fills the door, one hand on the frame and another on her hip. She looks me up and down, the way the policeman did twenty minutes ago. She comes close and starts smelling my clothes—a habit she's taken to since she started suspecting that I smoke.

She thinks my friends kept me.

"Those friends you've started hanging around with lately are going give us trouble, you'll see."

Her suspicions tend to dictate the course of my life.

She won't move from the doorframe until I offer her an explanation that satisfies her.

Or until I say I'm sorry.

"And don't use the rain as an excuse! You were due back home before it started raining!" she says sullenly.

Instead of answering I dump the bag on the floor and take off my jacket.

I didn't have the courage to talk about the assassination. I didn't have the strength or the willpower to share what I had seen. What could I say? How could I put into words something I hadn't yet taken in?

Mom takes the jacket from me angrily.

"What a way for a girl to dress! Come on, take your shoes off, I don't want the carpet ruined. And it's no use looking at me like that, like a lamb being led to the slaughter, don't give me that."

It annoys me to cry, even when no one is looking. I think it's a weakness; showing your cards to your opponent. But today I don't care. I can't hold back the tears, they stream down my face and I can't control them. I notice how warm they are because my face is so cold.

I wipe my feet on the doormat. I take my shoes off and give them to Mom.

She moves aside. I walk into the house. She closes the door—angrily, again. Then she heads for the bathroom holding my shoes, complaining all the way about my damn habit of leaving the house without an umbrella.

She returns with a towel. She's probably thinking that I've caught a cold, and I think her anger subsides somewhat as she rubs my head, back and chest with vigor.

"If you had at least worn your hooded jacket—but no, it's hopeless with you. It's our fault for letting you dress in rags like those good-for-nothing friends of yours."

"Mom," I say shivering.

"That's all we need now, for you to get sick. Take off those wet clothes immediately. We'll talk later."

I start taking my clothes off, but I have no strength. My underwear is wet too. Mom tells me to take everything off. I tell her I'm going to get some clean clothes.

"Go and have a shower—come on, it'll do you good."

I shake my head and tell her I don't feel like showering. I wear my bathrobe on top of the lukewarm underwear. It's the first comforting feeling I've had since the assassination.

I knew a shower would do me good, but I didn't want to be alone. I needed to talk, tell her what had happened, release what I had inside. But I couldn't: any words that arose from the whirlwind of my brain I discarded as insubstantial, irrelevant.

My head—I'm looking down a steep crevasse.

I hug Mom. She'll probably smell the cigarette smoke, but I don't care. I feel her warm breath on the back of my neck. Suddenly, she stops breathing. It feels like time has stopped.

She holds my head tightly against her chest and starts caressing my hair. I feel the warmth of her touch on my neck again; her hair tickles my nose.

The smell of newly applied perfume.

Suddenly, I let out a frightened cry: "They killed him!"

Mom stops caressing my head.

"Killed? Who do you mean?"

I told her what had happened. I remember we sat on the sofa. She kissed my eyes and my forehead. Then she gave me a handkerchief. I started drying my tears and crumpling the handkerchief; I couldn't stop.

The roar of a motorbike filled the room. Then there was silence again.

"My poor girl," Mom whispers over and over, and every now and then: "Thank God!"

She falls silent and makes a gesture in the air with her hand, as if what she'd been about to say had frightened her. She holds me by the elbow and stares into my eyes. Her voice is shaking a bit.

"At first I thought . . . that you . . . you know what I mean."

She goes quiet again, but I've understood. She doesn't need to mention that she's afraid of me being raped—I know that since I've grown up my mother's greatest fear is that I, her only daughter, will get raped. It worries her more than my good-for-nothing friends. She never mentions it but it's always there.

I nod. Yes, I know what she means.

She starts talking, measuring every word, trying to be as delicate as possible.

"That man . . . what you've seen . . . the shooting . . . things like that only cause pain. You must forget everything, my love. Promise me that you'll forget everything!"

4

She didn't mention the cigarette, although my clothes smelled of it. She didn't tell me off for being near the beach, even though she hated the idea of me being in that area after nightfall. She didn't ask me who I was with so late in the evening. Something I often thought came to my mind: that I had to make two lists. One with all the things that my mother forbade; the other with all the things she didn't like about me. If anyone ever looked at those two lists they would be able to see that everything was forbidden to me, and that my mother didn't like anything about me.

My mother had a fiery temper, though age has mellowed her, and I was not born to keep quiet—she says time has sharpened my tongue. Both of us were highly combustible; we could light fires and keep them going for a long time. It's true that we tended to patch things up quickly, but we never cleared up the whys and wherefores of our quarrels. The air was thick with old resentments and misunderstandings. But the curious thing is that the reasons for our fights—not so much for the ensuing resentment—were always pretty stupid, brought about mostly by my mother's need to improve on perfection. A sock found under my bed could start an argument any day. Silly things like that. She would start criticizing me with undue harshness: *You're careless, you haven't got a clue, you only care about your own things, you think what I do has no value.* I could be even harsher; the veins in my neck would swell like an opera singer's: *I'm sick of you, do you hear? Completely sick. Don't blame me just because you're frustrated.* At that point her brow would darken, she would push her hair back and, pressing her lips hard, would throw the sock on my bed with a disdainful look. She would then turn her back on me and leave my room.

She was great at playing the victim.

The thing is, even when Mom is caressing my hands I feel there's some sort of wall between us—a chasm that separates us more effectively than police crime scene tape.

"You must forget everything, my love. Promise me that you'll forget it all!"

It's easy to say that. But how can I forget? Is it possible to forget an assassination you've witnessed the way you may forget a book in the luggage net of a train, to relinquish such a memory to the net of forgetfulness?

I am alone, for the first time in my life. Mom's sentimental attitude won't ease this vertiginous feeling. An hour ago I saw a man get killed. How can I forget something like that? How can I make a promise I can't fulfill?

I look at her. She's a stranger. The serenity she emanated a few minutes ago is gone. Does she feel the distance between us too? I don't know. But I would say she intuits that something very out of the ordinary has just happened to us, because she starts to shift uncomfortably in the sofa.

She looks at the clock and shakes her head.

"Dad's late too; he should be here by now."

Silence. After a while, she starts talking about unimportant household matters. She doesn't want to be alone with me; she wants to fill up the time, but she doesn't know what else to say. She wants Dad to be here; she thinks it will be easier for her to cope with what's happened if the two of them are together.

"Should I put some music on?" she asks me, moving her hands and eyes exaggeratedly.

I shake my head no. Mom sighs, admitting defeat—she doesn't know what to do. But then her eyes suddenly light up: she has an idea. She stands up and, looking happy, says: "I know! Stay here, I'll be right back. I have a surprise for you."

She comes back very soon, carrying a long black dress on a hanger.

"Dad will tell me off for showing it to you before the December concert, but . . ." She doesn't finish the sentence.

A concert dress! At last, a long dress! How many times had I asked for it—but I had given up hope because my marks hadn't been great the previous semester.

"Come here, let's try it on."

She removes the dress from the hanger and holds it against my body to see if it's the right length. Excited, I remove my dressing gown and slip into the dress head first. I walk back and forth, as if I were on a catwalk, and when I turn around the skirt billows, swirling in waves around me. I do a few dance steps and run to my parents' bedroom to take a look at myself in the big mirror. It flatters my breasts. It fits my butt perfectly.

I see Mom standing behind me. She touches the dress, pulling here, straightening there. She's smiling, happy.

"You've lost weight lately and I was worried it would be too big."

She puts a pearl necklace around my neck. It isn't very long and the pearls are small. It looks beautiful with the black dress.

I look at myself in the mirror again. And then, suddenly, I remember the dark-haired man's pendant—the Basque cross. I see my face in the mirror, the involuntary frown that shows in my eyes and lips. Mom notices something.

"What's wrong? Don't you like it?"

I don't have the heart to burst her bubble. I turn around and kiss her.

"It's gorgeous, Mom, I love it. Thank you."

"Hurry now! Dad must be about to arrive!"

Many years have passed since. Fourteen. In that time very few people, apart from my relatives, have heard me talk about the assassination, and I've never made an effort to find out more about the man they killed. But that doesn't mean that I've forgotten the assassination, or the dead man for that matter. I've tried to forget, yes, but in vain. Memories aren't like clothes. You can put aside a skirt when it goes out of fashion, or when you get bored with it. You only need to want to. In these past fourteen years I've relived the scene of the assassination almost daily. Every morning when I glance through the papers, there's an item of news that opens the door to that moment. It could be news of a car bomb, or an interview with a victim, or the dismantling of a commando. There have been times when I have chosen to live without newspapers, but seeing the mother of someone who is in jail or a placard on the street can be enough to trigger the memory.

On such occasions it's the dead man's image that comes to mind—I suppose that's logical. But then, right

afterward, I feel the deep loneliness I felt that evening
with my mother; the same sharp sadness I felt as I con-
soled my mother because she couldn't console me.

It was a tender scene: me in my concert dress.

Me, alone.

5

I've spent more years alone than in a relationship. My life has been defined by the six or seven hours I spend playing the piano daily, and I've rejected everything that might come between me and that routine. I confess that I'm afraid of anyone noticing the cracks, and I confess that is the reason why I sometimes play without regard for those around me. Even so, it isn't easy. I know it costs me; I live with it every day—loneliness, I mean.

When I finished my music degree I decided I didn't want to follow the path of the music teacher, because I found the listless attitude of many of the music teachers I had met while studying for my degree sad and sterile. I thought of them as failures: they sacrificed their vocation to their daily bread. I started my professional career in a piano café. It wasn't a steady job, and I wasn't comfortable in that small-hour world. Also, it wasn't much of a challenge professionally. What I earned just about covered my expenses, but I refused to ask my parents for help.

I was about to give up when one day, at the café, I met the person who got me out of the financial hole I had dug myself into. After a performance, a young man came up to the piano to congratulate me. He said he worked on TV. We had dinner together that evening, and drank Armagnac from the same glass. The relationship was as beautiful as it was short-lived—it lasted fifteen days. I wouldn't bring this *amoureux de passage* into the story if it wasn't because it was he who opened the doors of TV

work for me. I got a slot playing a white piano on a talk
show, during the breaks between guests. This job lasted six
months. I was no trouble at all, and the producers must
have been happy with me, because they hired me for
another show. I worked on TV for almost five years, moving from show to show. I didn't have a permanent contract, but I was very grateful for the work—it was well
paid, and it created other opportunities. I made record-
ings, two on my own and another five or six playing with
bands. I also did summer concerts, and every now and
then orchestras asked me to play with them. Those were
my days of plenty. I managed to buy a beautiful apart-
ment. I didn't need anyone and, if I felt like it, I could
pick a lover any time. I never risked losing my independ-
ence.

I was sure it would be like that forever. But my
defense mechanism must have been weaker than I
thought. One day, while I was staying at a hotel in
Toulouse—I can't remember what sort of engagement
brought me there—I met the man with whom I ended up
sharing my life. He was a university professor and was
there for a conference. He was one of those interesting-
looking, dark, handsome men, with hair graying at the
temples. He was sweet to the eye and ear, a good conversationalist, and quite brave as well.

We used to feel a need to be together, a hunger, a
delight in having discovered each other. If we went to a
restaurant, or for a walk, he would take my hand in his
and, in a burst of high-flown tenderness, say: "I promise
thee, my lovely, I shall never be jealous of thy career." And
I would laugh a crystalline laughter, dazzled with youthful love.

We moved in together. It was a novelty: carefree sex; I floated in a state of spiritual well-being that did more good than damage to my career. My parents weren't very keen on our relationship—that was a good sign.

Even though until then I had been used to living on my own, I was happy to accept all aspects of life as part of a couple. I say all aspects, but it's difficult to believe now how naive I was. What happened was that at one point my lover ran out of admiration for me and my work. Bit by bit, the daily grind turned what had been so unique and dazzling into something insignificant. Another thing happened: the TV station had to cut corners, and I was one of the losers. I was on my way to the top but running out of chances. Fewer offers for concerts, fewer contracts—and in exchange, more hours at home in front of the piano. The sparks of love and pride disappeared from his eyes. By the time I realized this, he was far away— from my music as well as from me.

The state of perfect happiness lasted around ten months; routine kept us together four more years. A man is not seduced by the vision of his girl sitting in front of a piano, hour after hour, day after day.

Once, we went out for dinner (the financial trouble the TV station had gotten into was but a rumor in the papers at the time) and started talking about the difficulties couples with children face when they separate. We were sipping our after-dinner liqueur, not really engaged in the subject. Suddenly he said, "The woman gets the better deal, it's always the way, she ends up much better off than the man." I reacted like a cat that's just had a bucket of cold water thrown at it: what did he mean, to "end up better off"? What gave him the right to speak so categorically and use such cheap clichés? He brought up the case of a divorced man we both knew. Hadn't I heard him talk? He always said losing his children had caused him more pain than anything else in his life. Women like his wife would take the children as a form of revenge, to leave a dreadful void in the lives of their former partners. I didn't know the first thing about loneliness.

I felt like I'd been hit by lightning. Alone, lost, like the day when my mother asked me to forget everything I had seen: "That man . . . what you've seen . . . You must forget everything, my love. Promise me that you'll forget everything!"

I felt the cord that linked us together snap.

I was alone again, as on the day the man was killed.

He was still awaiting my answer, bringing the glass slowly to his lips. He thought he had won the dialectical battle. I was silent. He started talking aggressively, the way he did when he drank too much.

"You know what I dislike about you? That air of mystery you have. Like you're hiding something. I've always thought that." He emptied the glass in one gulp. "It's like you have a secret, and that secret raises you above everyone else."

I wanted to say something rude. I was very close to telling him all about the assassination: *I witnessed a man being killed, get it? I wasn't yet seventeen and there I was, facing a dead man, alone. And what do you know about loneliness? When have you ever been alone?* But I held back, because I was always wary of talking about it and I wasn't in the mood anyway. *I'll never tell you anything, you wouldn't understand a thing.* So instead of talking about myself and my memories I breathed deeply and changed the subject: often the feelings men experience during break-ups are more akin to melancholy than to loneliness;

melancholy, in order to last, needs to be fed by a sense of eternal loss; the unease men often feel when looking after their own children must be understood within that boundless melancholy, because when men confront their loss they also confront the fact that melancholy is over, and with it the need to worry about their children.

He banged the table with a fist. He spoke with hatred, drunkenly: it was impossible to have a normal conversation with me. He often used the word "normal" in relation to us, establishing what was normal in direct opposition to what we had going between us: we weren't a normal couple; it wasn't normal that we sacrificed everything to my career; one day we would have to speak about the things that bothered normal couples.

Children! The desire for children was at the root of such bitterness.

We were both in a mood. In the car, I looked out of the window for the entire length of the journey home. The morning after, however, he made love to me as if nothing had happened. He didn't even notice my unresponsiveness.

Despite all this, wanting to think that it wasn't too late yet, I started making special efforts to rebuild the channels of communication between us. At first I avoided all mention of his divorced friend or the distance between us. I thought maybe it was me, maybe only I felt we were growing apart. Later I tried to be more open, but did it with *sottigliezza*, as if I were playing the piano.

One evening, we were watching Clouzot's *Les Diaboliques* on TV. During one of the intervals he laughed and said: "You women, you're so tenacious! You never stop until you get what you want!"

It sickened me that he thought all women—especially me, of course—were comparable to the two cold and calculating women in the movie, but I waited until the film ended. I switched the TV off and told him we had to talk. About what, he asked. About what we needed to do to sort out our relationship.

Instead of confronting the problem he spoke in a wounded tone: "OK, you are going through a difficult period; sorry for being such poor help. What was it you were playing this morning? Come on!" And taking the cover off the piano, he urged me to play the score on the music stand, as if our problems could be solved by him taking some interest my work.

That killed off the last of my patience. I'm not capable of responding to stupidity with even more stupidity, so I escaped to the park in front of our house. I sat on a bench and started crying, without a thought for my belief that tears are a sign of weakness. I don't know how long I sat there. Slowly, I started to notice my surroundings. I saw an image partially blurred by my tears: on the bench next to me a woman sat gently rocking a pram.

Shortly afterward I saw my boyfriend. He walked as if against his wishes. He sat next to me and started to talk without taking his eyes off the pram. He didn't even look at me. He said he wanted to understand what was happening to me, that I had to talk to him, that I never gave him any clues. I didn't say anything. Still looking at the pram, he said he didn't know what else to say.

In the end he got bored, and proved to me what I already knew: he was incapable of showing his feelings without inflicting pain.

"Can't we be a normal couple?" his lips were trembling as he said this. "Your career, your career! You never think of anything else!" He yelled—something he hadn't done before. There was more rancor in his voice than ever.

"That's so low! The lowest you've been! And to think that I was ready to do anything, even consider children. You're so incredibly blind!"

He hadn't mentioned children, he said. It was true, and maybe I'd gone too far. But I didn't care, I knew his way with logic: he wouldn't confess to the unsaid, to the things his words implied. Too much trouble. In any case, what are *faux pas* but unconscious slips of the tongue?

Our story didn't last much longer. *C'est fini.* The palace we thought was built of stone was made of straw, and was vulnerable to rain and wind. It took five years for it to collapse.

He soon found another girlfriend. I went back to my old life. Solitude is difficult, but it feels safe, contrary to men's opinion.

In any case, now it embarrasses me to think that I gave those years of my life to such a worthless man, and it embarrasses me, too, to have dedicated so many words to someone like him now. There's only one possible justification—if I can call it that—for this long parenthesis: I was driven to it by my desire to talk about the loneliness I felt while talking to my mother on the day of the assassination, not the loneliness I've felt in the months since I parted from that man.

6

My mother helps me remove the black dress. I put the robe back on. Standing up, she holds up the dress and looks delighted.

"You'll be the best-looking girl at the November concert, you'll see." She's silent for a moment then winks at me—I'm her accomplice. "Be sure not to tell Dad that I've shown you the dress, OK?"

I smile back at her.

She leaves the living room carrying the dress on its hanger. I hear the key turn in the lock of my parents' closet. I'm calm, feel lighter: a heavy weight has been lifted from my shoulders. I breathe deeply and sigh. Mom is back from the bedroom and, hearing my sigh, thinks I'm terribly sad. She takes my hands and holds them tight against her breasts.

"Poor you, you're so unlucky!" it bursts out of her.

Unlucky! That word encapsulates her desire to console me, and her opinion, both inflexible and wrong, that I'm always looking for trouble, that I like complications. That I'm naive, kind-hearted, and will trust anyone; that in some way I'm not a normal person. I attract trouble, like the spire on a bell tower attracts lightning.

If I had walked home taking the path that led from the train station nothing would have happened to me. But on the day of the assassination I decided to walk toward the beach, it's as simple as that. It was an innocent decision based solely on my desire to meet the boy I had seen by the moving van. And that was that, pure chance. It marked my life.

It was I too who proposed we watch *Les Diaboliques*. And do you know why, Mom? Not because I wanted to quarrel with my boyfriend, clearly; it was just that I liked Simone Signoret a lot. Trivial decisions, taken for trivial reasons. But you've always thought that your daughter is a luckless simpleton. That I attract disaster. That I always fall for lost causes. The things that happen to me are no mere coincidences. You've always judged me; you've rarely shown me the kind of understanding that is expected from a mother. You even make me feel guilty because I've broken up with my boyfriend. I know I have my faults, but you only see my faults. "That's just how I am!" you've said whenever I've criticized you for being too harsh on me. However, I've never said, "Me too, that's how I am!" back to you. Because that isn't the point. Something about me exasperates you, and I'll never know what it is now, maybe because you don't know either. The fact remains that your need to criticize me has always made me feel at fault; guilty, though I don't know of what.

A key in the door. Mom lets go of my hands. The touching mother and daughter scene is cut short there and then.

"They've killed a dealer!" we hear Dad shouting from the doorway as he wipes his shoes on the mat.

Mom dries my eyes with the tips of her fingers. "Don't cry anymore; don't worry, I'll tell him what happened." She helps me tie up the robe and runs her fingers through my hair. "You look better now." I'm tired, I have no strength. I try to smile, though. Dad walks into the living room. Mom acts as if nothing has happened, and I don't know what to do.

He stands in the middle of the living room, sensing that something is off-key. His hesitation lasts the time it takes him to glance at us. He takes his jacket off, hangs it from the corner of a shelf and faces Mom, all the time talking ceaselessly:

"I'm sure you know who he is. This guy who's all skin and bones; he runs a dingy bar near the port. He's got this big ugly dog that's always by his side—just in case, I guess, otherwise why have it? You must have seen him around."

Trying to protect me, Mom is gesturing at him to shut up. Dad puts one foot on the raised fireplace and undoes his shoelaces. He hasn't noticed Mom's gestures. And if he has seen them he hasn't understood their meaning.

"He wasn't a local, his nickname was Toloxa, like the city," Dad continues, "a small-time crook, one of those lazy, immoral guys who acts as a link between traffickers. See where that's got him!"

He takes off his other shoe and leaves them both by the fireplace, next to each other. It's a mechanical gesture—the fire hasn't been lit.

"Haven't you seen all those posters against drug dealers? The town is full of them. This time it was this unlucky bastard, next time . . ."

That damned *unlucky* again! I'm about to say something. But Dad keeps jabbering on: "They say he'd been to jail lots of times. But it was just the usual: out in two days. On the streets again, peddling that shit, those drugs . . ." He pauses to breathe. "Well, there'll be no more of that kind of . . ."

"Oh God, don't be so stupid!" Mom shouts at him.

Her shout shocks him into silence. He's paralyzed for a few seconds, discomforted by the thought of his inappropriateness. When he speaks again, he sounds slightly miffed: "It's just a manner of speaking. I meant to say that he's dead. You don't believe that I approve of that sort of barbarity, do you? I don't like drug dealers, but that doesn't mean anything."

My mother has a beautiful voice, crystalline and full of tonalities. But she practically snarls when she interrupts Dad's lecture:

"Have you seen your daughter? Will you look at her at least!"

They both look at me. Silence.

I broke down in floods of tears. Mom knew what had happened, but Dad could only watch an astonishing scene unfold: his daughter in her bathrobe, wringing a handker-chief dementedly, eyes red and streaming, hair wet and entangled.

Dad didn't know how to react; his eyes darted from left to right hoping to find something that would throw light on the reason for all this, but he didn't say a word. He didn't like what he was seeing, and he needed some time to adjust to it, to define it. Suddenly his jaw dropped, as if he had thought of something atrocious, as if he were about to say, "It can't be!"

Half an hour earlier, it had been Mom who had mis-interpreted my arriving home drenched and wretched. It looked like Dad too was coming to the conclusion that his only daughter, his little girl, had been raped. It must have looked like that.

Dad raised his eyebrows and with a lost look asked, "What happened?"

Mom, answering my wordless plea, started telling him what had happened to me. She went straight to the

point, using no unnecessary words. When she mentioned
words like shots or dead or blood she looked at me as if to
ask forgiveness ("it can't be avoided, my darling"). She was
repeating everything I had said, remembering every little
detail and using almost the same words. But I felt dissoci-
ated from her retelling; it felt distant, cold. It was like
what she was saying had happened to someone else, not to
me.

Before she finishes, Dad looks at me with a stupid
smile, unable to say a word. He breathes deeply, as if the
news he has just heard has dispersed an awful premonition.

He comes toward me slowly. He puts a hand on the
nape of my neck and brings me toward him. He kisses my
forehead. Then my lips. A powerful emotion shakes me, I
feel it all the way from my mouth to my feet—it's the first
time Dad has kissed me on the lips.

Then he holds my elbow delicately, with infinite care,
as if I were made of very fine glass. We look at each other.

Life is strange. Mom had listened to me with all her
heart, she had sat me on her lap, we had embraced for a
long time; Dad had been clumsy and thoughtless, and
then he had given me a kiss on the lips. And I was grateful to him. But what about Mom? Even before Dad died
I often thought hard about the reason for the difference
between my feelings for them, and all I was able to come
up with was this: the details make the difference, not the
obvious demonstrations of love.

"Did anyone see you?" he asks suddenly. "I mean
someone who might know you."

Dad's question terrifies me, because it forces me to
relive the scene. I close my eyes. I hear the sounds of sirens
and people's prattle, but those who emerge from the shadows illuminated by the camera's flashes have no faces,

known or unknown. Even the photographer has no face.
Only the dead man's features are etched on my brain.

"No, I don't think so. At least I don't remember."

"And you? Did you see anyone?"

I stare at him; I don't understand the question.

"I mean the killer. The man who shot him. Or his
accomplice. Did you see anyone's face?"

"No!" I scream.

"Good. Better that way. You've been through
enough, darling, I don't want anyone coming to ask you
questions."

My state of mind, my parents' attitude, life itself: it
seems everything is reverting to its natural order. What I
experienced so vividly and dramatically an hour and a half
ago is now part of the past; all the events surrounding the
assassination are becoming more and more blurred; it feels
like it was a dream, seeing the drug dealer get killed, not
like something that really happened.

As a child I had a puppet theater. Grandma had given
it to me on my birthday. It came with a big castle and ten
straw marionettes. I would play the king, because he had a
scepter he could use to punish everyone. Whenever I got
angry with anyone in the house I turned them into the
maid or the thief or the soldier of the castle, and happily
brought the scepter down on their backs. "Take this and
this and this, you're bad, bad, bad." I would hit them mer-
cilessly, until I got tired and said, "There, dead now!" I
didn't have a speck of what we normally call bad conscience, even when the dead marionette was Mom or Dad.

More sad than angry with myself, I start putting
together the face of the dead man: the salt-and-pepper
hair, the bags under the eyes, the tobacco-stained
teeth . . .

7

"Am I the only one thinking about dinner in this house?" says Dad from the kitchen door, in a tone that tries to be cheerful. "I'll get changed and come right back."

Mom removes the vase from the center of the table. Then, taking the tablecloth, shakes it vigorously in the air. There is nothing surprising in that mundane gesture. Mom, like Dad, is trying to coat everything she does with the veneer of normality; and me, too—as I watch the cloth being spread over the table, I go behind the kitchen door and take the bread from its bag, as I normally do. I take the bread knife and the breadbasket and slice and watch as the pieces of bread pile up in the basket, as I normally do.

Dad is in the kitchen again, he's changed clothes. "What do I do?" Mom hands him some tomatoes. Dad turns on the faucet to wash them. In that instant, the telephone rings in the other room. Mom signals with her head for Dad to pick it up. He leaves the tomatoes by the sink and goes to pick up the phone. "Hello, who is this?" He's quiet for a while. "Yes, I've heard." And he closes the door to the room with his leg; he doesn't want me to hear.

Mom keeps moving: she washes the tomatoes. She slices them and puts them on plate. Leaving the knife, she takes the rubbish bin from under the sink and leaves it on the floor. The tomato cores go into the bin. Then she starts whisking salt, vinegar, and olive oil.

Mom had been silent since she told Dad what had happened. She was probably going over it ceaselessly in her mind—wondering what to tell me, how best to deal with me. She kept darting from one end of the kitchen to the other, never once stopping; it's well known that keeping busy makes restlessness more bearable. She washed the dishes she had used to make dinner; she ran a damp cloth across the sink and the surrounding area, then grabbed the broom and swept up the breadcrumbs that had fallen on the ground. She didn't say a word to me the whole time, or glance in my direction; it was as if concentrating on the job at hand could release her from having to say or demonstrate anything to me. Every now and then she looked at the door. So now it was Dad's turn to deal with me, was that it? Mom would do nothing until he returned to the kitchen.

Mom has an easy disposition; her problem is that she is incapable of showing affection. The need to appear proper at all times is stronger than she is. I have often thought that it must be hard to give up who you are and take on a role for the rest of your life, hard and tiresome: always having the right words and the appropriate reactions ready, always being the paradigm of exemplary behavior. Perhaps it's caused by insecurity, I don't know. Even though Mom rejected religion in her youth, she has embraced the stereotypical female and mother roles dictated by her religious education, like her mother and grandmother before her. The only difference is that her ancestors acted according to their faith—a system without cracks. Mom and her unfortunate generation, however, were slaves to the rules of a long-gone ideology. That was why she would get angry with me: as soon as I demanded a reason for any of her decisions we were sure to have an altercation. One of her strategies for winning arguments was authoritarianism. The other was to play the victim. As on previous occasions, she is angry with me—but now she only pouts and acts victimized. She knows I can't put up with authoritarianism right now. In any case, she continued to exercise both strategies with great dexterity until the day Dad died.

She brings the plate with the tomatoes to the table. But the table hasn't been set yet, and that's my job. Even so, she doesn't dare ask me to do anything; she doesn't want to hurt me. So she makes a gesture: the table hasn't been set. I almost trip on the rubbish bin as I walk to the cupboard to get the plates. She knows Dad and I dislike having the rubbish bin on the floor, but she always puts it there. An astonishing habit, considering she's the sort of person who cleans what's already clean. Is it that odd, though, that to escape her compulsion to be in absolute control of everything she allows herself this sole, tiny expression of slovenliness?

I'm putting the plates on the table. Mom is warming up the cod. Dad is still on the phone. There are some old-fashioned French expressions on the parchment-colored tablecloth, written one after the other in green, stylized letters. I sit down and move my plate slightly to one side. I trace my fingers through the lines of words. *A la recoquillette, au beuf violé, au cassepot.* My parents bought it on a trip to Bordeaux once. *A myremimofle, a la tirelitantaine, a mouschart.* Dad has asked here and there, tried to find out where the expressions come from. No one has been able to solve the query. Dad says they sound like the names of children's games. Who knows. There are sixteen of them altogether. I know them by heart and repeat them to myself like a litany, even though I don't know what many of them mean. *A pimpompet, a cochonnet va devant, a ventre contre ventre, a la vergette.* A great form of entertainment to indulge in while waiting for food, it avoids fights and helps me ignore my parents' arguments. *Au pinot, a laver la coiffe Madame, a cul sallé, a rouchemerde,* and my finger stops dead at the next expression, *au juge vif et juge mort,* but my eyes and my memory move on to the last one, *a male mort,* and I take my hand off the tablecloth quickly, as if I'd gotten an electric shock. There it is again, the recent nightmare, it did happen: *a male mort, a male mort, a male mort!* A dead man. Blood drips from the stylized green letters; it runs in quick rivulets, spreads all over the tablecloth.

"Are you OK?" asks Dad when he returns from his telephone conversation.

I close my eyes, breathe in, open them. There's no blood on the tablecloth.

"It's nothing. I'm fine. Really."

And to prove that I am well I put a slice of tomato in my mouth. I feel sick. My stomach is empty, I haven't eaten since lunchtime, but I can't eat a thing. I swallow the slice of tomato without chewing it, in one gulp, and drink water to force it down. I take a second slice, help it down with water again.

I had to appear brave: *I'm OK, really, I'm not obsessed, these things happen often, it's happened to me, so what, it's not particularly important, having witnessed an assassination by accident, don't go overboard.* Since childhood, my parents had always tried to protect me excessively against all sorts of little problems. Is this the plight of the only child? I don't wish it on anyone. You might think me spoiled, but for me, being an only daughter was full of disadvantages. The advantages were few and treacherous.

I realized that I couldn't show weakness: *I'm brave, can't you see? I'm fine, really.* Because if I did they would suffocate me. Their intentions would be good, but they would suffocate me.

Mom starts chatting about everything and nothing, sometimes interrupting Dad, sometimes addressing me.

"They said it'll rain again tomorrow. I hope I can grab a moment around lunchtime to do the shopping. Are you going to trim your beard? I'm going to Mom's later, her iron's broken down. I'm sure she kept pressing and pressing buttons until it broke."

He plays her game, and, feigning interest, elaborates on the subjects she brings up. You've had the misfortune of witnessing an assassination, my pet, I know, but let's pretend nothing's happened.

Please, continue with the performance. I don't care. In fact, right now I prefer this enactment; it is too tiresome to say "I'm OK" every five minutes.

Suddenly, it occurs to me to bring up an old, contentious subject; I want to turn this moment of infinite love to my advantage. Am I not under the influence of a terrible shock? At least I want them to know that I won't give up until I go to the conservatoire. They won't go against my wishes, at least not today. For once I'll have my say!

"Have you decided whether I'm to continue going to school or apply for a place at the conservatoire?" I ask brusquely.

Mom looks at Dad. Dad hems and haws. Obviously, he's thinking about how to phrase his answer.

They signed me up for piano lessons at the music academy before I turned seven. It looked pretty; I can't think of a better explanation for their decision to have me play the piano. It was so elegant to have a single, spoiled daughter like me who played the piano. It helped them conform to a certain social class, to have a certain style, to exude recognizable charm; it enabled them fulfill the stereotype of having a girl who was brought up to be decorative. But they had to recognize at last that I had gone way beyond the stereotype: I loved the piano and couldn't envisage a future without it. My first serious confrontations with my parents started because of this. Every time I spoke about wanting to go to the conservatoire they postponed the decision to a later date. Your studies come first, they said. And what about my piano studies, what are they? I would answer. Whenever they wanted me to impress their friends or relatives they would overwhelm me with praise and plead with me to play: "You don't want to make us look bad, do you?" It looked so pretty to have their only daughter play the piano at their parties. They never encouraged me to take my music career further; in their plans for my future the piano was only a pretty accessory. I checked once. I told them I wanted to leave the music academy and needed them to sign a form allowing me to do so. Dad was non-committal, as ever: "It's up to you, but you should think it over before you make your mind up." Mom's reaction was much more practical: "She plays so well already. She could just continue playing what she knows at home." I never brought home the form from the academy, and, after a week, a passing comment I heard from Dad settled the issue: "It seems she's enjoying it again, don't you think?"

My question hangs in the air; my parents are still in shock.

"What do you say? You know I want to go to the conservatoire," I say as naturally as I can.

"Well, what's wrong with continuing at the music academy? That way you can combine high school with music," says Dad.

"Dad!" I complain; if only he knew how much that old argument bores me. "You know the conservatoire is the only place where I can get a music degree."

"And leave your studies? Look, it's important to learn about all sorts of things in life, you'll have plenty of time later on to decide what you want to concentrate on. Besides, you know your piano teacher isn't so sure about you going to the conservatoire."

"But I could get a degree in music! You promised!"

"True, but we have to take your teacher's opinion into account, don't you think?" he said, making a ball of the piece of bread he held between his fingers.

My teacher! If I'm making a living off music nowadays it's certainly not thanks to my teacher. She never showed any signs of believing in my talent. Every time she heard the conservatoire mentioned she felt threatened; people gossiped, they said it was because she didn't want competition. But I don't think so. At least I don't think that was the only reason. She was old-fashioned and she liked it: she put her hair up in a bun, wrapped a silk scarf around her neck, pinned a golden brooch to her breast. Her skirts always came below the knees. She used make-up to disguise her age. It was clear to me that my teacher was also one of those people who loved playing the piano because it looked pretty, and the girls who wanted to take it further than decorativeness made her uncomfortable.

"Come on, let's leave this subject for another time; we don't need to make the decision today," says Mom, putting a special emphasis on the word today to underline that *today* nothing is as it should be.

Dad looks at his watch. Saying it's time for the news, he stands up to leave the table. Mom's eyes are like burning bullets. Realizing he's put his foot in it, he starts making excuses:

"I'll be right back. I want to see what footage they have. Just in case." He looks at me. "I hope you're not in it!"

Dad heads toward the living room, down the corridor.

Without a word, I leave the table too.

"Where are you going?" Mom pleads more than asks; she doesn't want me to go with him.

I hesitated for a moment. I was drawn to the idea of watching what had happened on TV. But what did I expect to see? The TV would only show the rigmarole surrounding the scene of the assassination: speechifying politicians, surprised neighbors, the chief of police making a statement; that would be all. I wanted to relive something that the TV would never show: the mute connection between the dead man and me. So I had two options: I could go against my mother and get angry at myself while sitting in front of the TV, or I could seek consolation elsewhere.

"To play the piano!" I say snappily.

I'm sure Mom takes my fury for distress.

8

I switch on the lamp and tilt it toward the music stand. Before resting on the score—Schumann's *Scènes d'enfants*—the light moves across the old family photographs on the piano. Dad's family refers to the display as the cemetery.

It was the first chance I had to be by myself since I came home. I had been waiting for this moment all through dinner. I needed to be alone to put my thoughts in order. But anger clouded my head; I couldn't think calmly. I was incensed, it's true, but not because Dad had gone against me in the discussion about my studies. I was angry with myself because I had acted like a despicable, calculating person: I had tried to use the tenderness brought on by my having witnessed an assassination to get my way.

I had said what needed to be said. But at what price?

I felt nauseous again, but this time it had nothing to do with an unchewed slice of tomato.

I start playing though I still haven't controlled my anger. First, some very quick scales to get rid of the stiffness. As I move, my body casts flittering shadows on the black piano, on the old pictures, on the white wall.

Then I start playing *Bonheur parfait*—in bursts, to let my fury out, without regard for the delicate balance of the two hands. When I finish the piece I look at the clock: fifty-two seconds. Maria-João Pires' version—which is the one we use as a blueprint at the academy—lasts one minute and seven seconds. I've speeded it up by fifteen seconds, and the piece barely lasts a minute!

I start the metronome and breathe deeply to calm myself down. I crack my fingers. Closing my eyes, I begin to play the first few *pianissimo* bars. All my senses are focused on the movement of my fingers—I want my left hand to do a good job. I navigate the moment when the emphasis of the melody shifts from the right to the left hand without a glitch, the change of tone that follows is clean and flawless, and after the part where the notes go at a trot, I finish the piece's last few bars at a measured pace. One minute and five seconds. So close to the model, and no obvious faults! I start playing for the third time, without the metronome.

The result was the same, with just a couple of seconds' difference. I was amazed: finally, I had mastered *Bonheur parfait!* The happiness I felt then is crystallized in my memory, because it was crucial to my development as a pianist. At that precise moment, and through practice, not theory, I realized the meaning of a metaphor my teacher often used: "Instinct is the lover of technique." Then her hands would flutter near her heart and she would say: "The artistic expression reflects the nature of their relationship." For me, the day the man was killed that metaphor lost its verbal quality and became something physical, something I felt in my flesh: instinct and technique intertwined in my very fingers.

Then it was time for *Historie bizarre,* another lively piece from *Scènes d'enfants.* My hands moved across the keys of their own accord: instinct and technique, dancing. Then I had a strange thought I have recalled often. The piano is an animal, a beautiful, silky-haired dog. I caress it; I throw a stick for him to fetch and the dog jumps in the air and clasps it between his teeth. Afterward, he sits on his hind legs and wags his tail gratefully—right, left, right, left—like a metronome.

Since then, if I have to give a concert and feel nervous, I look at the piano as if it were a dog standing in front of me. I treat the piano as I would a loyal dog: we talk, I pat him, tapping the keys lightly—*à promener, à promener!* We even go for walks.

For many years, I never told anyone about this. I broke the rule one day, after giving a concert in a small theater in Bilbao. It was shortly before I split up with my boyfriend. I was happy because I felt the concert had gone very well. We drank champagne in the hotel bar, and in our room, hoping to thaw the atmosphere between us, and with the help of the champagne bubbles, I told him about seeing the piano as a dog. Today the piano responded like a loyal dog, were my words. He laughed coarsely and said, "What does the dog do when you play a wrong note, then? Does he bark, bite, or crap?

I'm a moron, I told myself, that's what I get for trying to fix the unfixable.

Just then someone comes into the piano room and I feel two hands rest on my shoulders: my mother—I recognize her touch. I finish *Historie bizarre* and, almost without pause, start playing *Bonheur parfait* again—I don't want to ruin my concentration, but also, I need to disguise the fact that Mom's gesture has moved me.

When I finish the piece I look at the clock. One minute thirteen seconds. This time I played it more slowly—still, I'm happy with the result.

Quietly, Mom whispers: "Is that the piece you were having so much trouble with?" When I nod, she says: "You played it really well. I mean it."

I turn my head to smile at Mom and see Dad by the door. He's calmer after watching TV. Smiling, he tells me, "There were no witnesses; they just said so. You weren't in the report. That's the most important thing. No one will bother you."

Dad's words destroy the magic of the moment. But I smile at him anyway, and open another score. Mom takes one of the pictures from the family cemetery and, with the edge of her apron, removes specks of dust only she can see from the glass and frame. She does exactly the same with every single photograph. Then she looks at Dad, and they leave for the kitchen. I hear them talk. The piece I'm playing is easy and I don't need to press the damper to listen to what's going on in the kitchen.

"They didn't say much. That he was divorced. And that he was a small-time drug dealer," I hear Dad say. "But the images they showed were from quite a while after the assassination—they were putting the body in a coffin. From way after she left the scene, at any rate. We can relax, no one knows anything."

"People always know," Mom snaps at him.

"Do you think the TV guys would have left anything unsaid if they knew more? They'd have taken the opportunity to blur the lines, as usual."

I can't hear Mom's answer to that. But I hear what Dad says next:

"They're scum. Their tongues won't get rusty, oh no. And they're left-leaning, and liberal, of course, but when it comes to the crunch, if they actually wreck someone's life they'll tell you"—and he changes his voice, as if he were imitating someone—"'we're here to safeguard freedom of information.'"

Dad talks and talks—his mouth is full now. He's probably eating some cheese, because I hear a familiar complaint:

"No, leave it there, please; I'll have one last tot."

Dad went through the same ritual almost every night: when Mom tried to remove the bottle of wine from the table, he demanded one last drink to help down a piece of cheese; softly, but he always demanded that last tot.

I hear the thump of the bottle returning to the table.

"Politicians, journalists; all scum. The number of bastards we feed! Not to mention the other idiots, the ones who think they're going to save the world." Mom asks him to lower his voice, but to no avail. "Heartless bastards! How could they kill someone in front of a child?"

I am the child. The terrorists are bastards.

But other assassinations happened before I witnessed this one, and Dad never used words such as bastard. He did use it to describe the dead man ten minutes before, though, with no qualms. How many times had I heard him say things like *He must have done something!* I too unquestioningly accepted that "he must have done something." My problem was that I was the reason my Dad had called the terrorists bastards for the first time.

One day, eight months ago, when I spent my days looking after Dad at the hospice, the regular TV schedule was suddenly interrupted by news of another terrorist assassination. We were quiet for a long while. Suddenly, he blurted out, "How many years of this! We were very frightened for you, you know, we didn't want you to get involved in all that." He followed this with a short speech against hatred, issued with tired vehemence. His cancer was terminal by then. "Hatred is like fire," he said, "the harder it burns, the more fuel it demands." I mentioned how I heard him say "bastards!" that time at the kitchen table. He didn't remember, but he seemed embarrassed that I had mentioned it. When he answered, he spoke more seriously than if he were dictating his will: "We use words to build our little worlds for our own convenience, without caring that we may well be destroying someone else's world in the process."

Bang! I hear a dry explosion. The fright makes me stop playing. My parents stop talking. More explosions; loud noises. Fireworks! They're very close. Around Moila, I think. It must be some sort of celebration.

But suddenly, I'm gripped by a dark thought. What if . . . No, it can't be. I can't believe that there may be people out there celebrating this man's death.

I jump from the piano stool as if it were on fire. I run to the bathroom, kneel in front of the toilet bowl and vomit. The slices of tomato look exactly the same as when they went in. That's all there is.

Just as I'm about to stand up, I feel my mother's hand on my forehead. She wants to hold my head. I turn sideways and, removing her hand from my forehead, tell her:

"It's over, Mom. I'm better now."

"What you need is some warmth in your body: a hot shower and a cup of really hot chamomile tea—that's exactly what you need," she says, turning on the hot water tap.

I came out of the shower feeling renewed. I wiped the steam from the mirror and, instead of a brush, ran a fine comb through my hair, not giving a damn about the knots or pulling my own hair. Afterward, I spent some time examining my face. When I compare my face as it is now with the pictures I keep of that time, I realize I haven't changed much. I still look the same as the girl in the mirror, if you discount the wrinkles around the mouth and eyes. But that night I thought I looked older. I got frightened by this older version of myself, and though I laugh about it now, the truth is that fear made me do something strange: I took a towel and threw it over the mirror.

9

I prop my pillow against the headboard and sit back. I rub my eyes. Everything in the room looks the same. Next to the bed, my bedside table; on it, the lamp painted green. In front of me, a big poster I bought in the hippie shop in the port: Iggy Pop, naked from the waist up. Mom doesn't like it at all. That's why it's there. My desk is under the poster—full of textbooks, folders, colored pencils, and notebooks. My soaked socks are laid out to dry on top of the radiator.

I switch the light off so my parents think I'm about to go to sleep. I hear the clinking of coffee cups in the living room. I think they're sitting on the sofa. They must be whispering, because I can't hear them talk.

Go and talk to her! Mom says between sobs. Dad, however, tries to soothe her: *She's calm, isn't she? Let's not upset her now. Besides, what can I tell her?* Mom persists: *You'll think of something. She could do with one of your little talks; you know she always pays more attention to you.*

Even if I'm only guessing what my parents are saying, I know that Mom often reproaches Dad for our complicity. She'll say things like, *You've ganged up on me, haven't you?* Or, *You deal with her!*

I often wondered what my parents' relationship was like. I don't think they were just keeping up appearances, because they both got very upset when they argued. However, their personalities were completely opposed. Mom has always been all about order, control, and pragmatism; you would think her only concern was perfection. Dad, on the other hand, always acted like chumminess and good vibes could solve everything. Sparks flew when the two attitudes were taken to the extreme. I seldom saw them take their quarrels to a point where they would say terrible things to each other; but when they did, they unleashed all their inner poison on each other. Afterward they'd both go mute. They'd be embittered and full of bile, but said nothing. They'd give each other evil looks, though. At times like those the atmosphere was unbearable.

On such occasions I would think the worst: I would imagine them divorced, angry at each other, living separate lives. The mere thought of having to choose between my mother and father sent me to the piano to relieve my unease. My fingers would make the keys twinkle; I would sing to myself. I don't speak German, so I would sing the French versions of Schumann's melancholy airs. To this day, *Lorsque j'ai le coeur lourd* and *Qui me délivrera des attaches de ce monde?* remain my favorites. It's always Schumann. I don't know of anyone who does melancholy as well as him. It was even more difficult when Mom and Dad made up, though, because I couldn't stand the sickly sweetness that followed their battles. Their nauseating smiles and secret whisperings made me feel like a third wheel; they would hardly notice my presence.

I was in their way. I didn't exist.

If only you knew what a good time I'd have without you! I would think to myself; and in my mind, I punished them just like I'd done with the puppets as a child.

I don't remember how long I remained like that, observing my room. I don't even know if I fell asleep. What I know is that after a while I could only hear street noises,

and I was lying down, not leaning against the headboard.
I pulled the blanket up to my chin. I did it mechanically.
I didn't really need to; the smell of paint so common to
radiators that have just been turned on told me that mine
was on. For the first time that autumn. At some point,
Mom's sense of guilt had won over her thriftiness.

Thinking that Mom and Dad were probably in bed,
I turned the light on and looked at the clock. I took a
book from the bedside table and started to read. I don't
remember the title or the author, but I remember the
cover. It was sky blue. The picture showed a hand holding
a paintbrush, painting the sky above an idyllic seascape.

One page. Another. The letters seemed to travel in
flocks, like starlings in fall. But even though my eyes were
wide open and I wasn't sleepy, I couldn't concentrate; I
couldn't retain what I was reading, and I often went back
to reread a passage—like a walker who, near the summit,
realizes the path has vanished.

Just then, the handle creaks. The door opens. I see it's
Dad and relax.

"I saw the light was on and . . ." he apologizes.

I gesture for him to come in, and close the book. Dad
comes over and fixes the bedclothes around me. Then he
sits at the edge of the bed.

"Can't you sleep?" he says in a very mellow voice. He
asks if I'd like a drink: water, chamomile, warm milk?

I lean sideways to look at him, leaning on my elbow.
Instead of answering his question, I tell him, "Well,
Dad . . . I hope things won't go beyond . . ."

Sensing my worry has made him alert. He doesn't say
anything, but he holds my hand tight.

"I don't want anyone at school to know anything. If they knew . . ." I leave the sentence unfinished, unable to explain how scared I am of my schoolmates' gossip.

My schoolmates didn't witness a terrorist assassination. I did. They didn't hear the shots, feel the sound of the man's body hitting the ground, didn't see the blood. I did. Their lack of feeling toward the dead—the same I myself had shown often, in fact—and my present state of mind were so diametrically opposed: how would I react to their stupid comments? How could I not respond to their arrogance? I only needed to remember how little the assassinations I had heard about on TV had bothered me until then, the carelessness with which I would swiftly change channels before being confronted with such news. Terrorist assassinations didn't take place in my world, they never touched me, they weren't like Grandpa's death. To me, they were unreal. Far removed. They belonged in television. Police controls and tanks were different, they were familiar—I saw them often on my way to school. I knew that the two different images were part of the same situation, of course, but I hadn't linked cause and effect. Only the tanks seemed obvious to me.

"They don't need to know. Nobody needs to know. There was nothing on TV, you know that," Dad says emphatically.

"People always know," I retort, and just then realize that I am repeating the very words Mom used a couple of hours ago.

He starts cleaning the nails of one hand with the other hand's nails. He always does that when he runs out of arguments or doesn't know what else to say. Finally, he says in a voice full of uncertainty:

"If you don't say anything . . . If you don't mention it to anyone . . . It's in your hands, isn't it?"

Dad knew that it wasn't just up to me; you didn't need to be a genius to realize that many people had seen me standing in front of the dead man. But that was typical of Dad; he always got stuck for arguments in serious discussions. He was good with words, a great, lively conversationalist. Unless the conversation was serious. Then he would dither, unable to come up with anything to say. You'd think that for him, talking about disagreeable things made them worse.

"Actually, it isn't in my hands," is what I thought, remembering all the people who had come to see the dead man.

"And what if someone recognized me?"

"If someone actually did, they would only have seen you among other people. No one can actually say you witnessed his death. Only we know that: you, Mom and I."

Dad half-closes his eyes suddenly; it looks as like he is dwelling on some profound thought. After a while, he holds my hand and says, "The smartest thing to do is go on as usual. Go to school and continue with your normal life, as if nothing had happened." He fixes a tiny smile on his lips. "Don't worry. This'll be our secret. And it'll stay with us, within these walls."

He's waiting for my answer. I nod and offer him a forced smile. You'd think that it was I who was consoling him, and not the other way around.

Dad gives me a kiss. On the cheek. Then he stands up and brushes invisible threads off his trousers.

Mom comes into the room, as if Dad's brushing his legs had been some sort of signal. She brings a glass of milk on a plate. Next to the glass, half of a small pill.

"It'll help you sleep."

I look at her with surprise; Mom is usually terrified of tranquilizers.

"Don't worry; half a Diazepam just this once won't harm you."

Dad nods in agreement.

I put the pill in my mouth. It tastes bitter. I drink some milk.

"Call if you need us, OK?" they say from the door. Then they close it slowly, quietly.

I lay there, looking at the ceiling with my eyes open; not asleep and not awake either.

Stupid, you're so stupid! Why did you have to walk by the beach instead of the train station? You knew already what sort of place that is! You've seen with your own eyes the kind of trash that comes out of that bar—but no, you had to go that way!

I switch off the lights and curl under the sheets. They are cold. They feel a bit rough, the way linen does after it's been washed, and smell of the lavender scent Mom mixes with the soap when she does the laundry.

I link my hands and hide them between my knees. I close my eyes, ready to enjoy the smell of lavender. But the pale face of the dead man won't let go of me. He looks at me accusingly: *Won't you help me get up from the ground?* Or maybe he's demanding justice: *It was a mistake, I'm no drug dealer; I've never done anything wrong!* His pale face has no intention of leaving my sheets, or shutting up for that matter, and when he speaks, he sprays me with saliva.

Suddenly, the smell of vanilla is stronger than the smell of lavender.

I stick my head out from under the sheets. Then take out my hand and switch the light back on. Everything that happened earlier floods into my mind, down to the smallest detail; I relive everything.

Since that day, I have often tried to write down the details of the assassination. Mostly in the hope that it would drive the memory away. But I always gave up after writing a few lines. It was pointless. I never even finished a whole sentence. So I would leave it at that. At times because I couldn't gather the courage to do it; at other times because I doubted anyone would be interested in my thoughts; but mostly because I wasn't brave enough to act freely. *Maybe one day,* I would say to myself. I started making notes, without much hope they would ever amount to anything. I wrote down sensations, impressions, events: empty mnemonic sentences. There were more random specific notes about the death itself than notes about the effect the death had on me. And of all the specifics, the one I always returned to was the smell of vanilla. I once asked a gardener friend of mine which flower smelled of vanilla. He showed me a plant that is not common here and said it was a heliotrope. It had clumps of violet flowers and smelled of vanilla; the smell was very similar to the one emanating from the flowerpot next to the dead man. But it didn't trigger any memories.

That day I decided I wouldn't write about what happened. Who was I, after all? Nothing special had happened to me; I wasn't the protagonist of any event. I didn't die, I've never been raped, I'll never play the piano at the New York Metropolitan. My life is not particularly interesting to anyone other than myself and those who love me. And the fact that I witnessed an assassination is my own private matter.

Those were my thoughts, more or less. But then, a few months ago, as I was glancing through the paper looking for an announcement for a piano recital I was giving, I noticed a small article about a man who had just left jail. I wouldn't have paid much attention to the article or the names if my dead man's name hadn't been mentioned alongside the free man's. The assassin was out; in the eyes of the law he had paid his dues. And the man I had seen dead, hitting the ground, was fourteen long years under the cold earth now, under a tombstone.

10

Wind and rain rattle the window. I open my eyes. The room is in darkness; I feel like I have slept a lot. I switch on the lamp on the bedside table and look at my alarm clock. Only a few minutes before the alarm goes off. I rub my eyes to prove to myself that this is me, that I am awake, that these are my eyes. It must be cold outside: the windows are steamed up. Despite this, the room feels as warm as it did last night.

I pull the blankets up to my chin and stare at the ceiling for a while.

It's another day, you've slept all night, I tell myself. You've had a dreamless, uninterrupted night's sleep. Yesterday's events are far away; someone else, not you, happened to walk by when the assassination took place; that must be what happened, because it feels like yesterday's memories belong to someone else. But you're shocked by the profound impact the dead man has had on you, how something that happened so quickly can affect you so much. You would like to forget this thing that is nailed to your memory; you don't want to know who the dead man is, whether he had a family, what his hopes in life were. He was a crook, a small-time dealer, and your parents don't like that part of town; there are lots of drugs around there—that's all you know. And you don't want to know much more; it might give you a bad time if you did. It wouldn't be good to fill your head with dark thoughts, you know your tendency to fight lost causes would take over. You don't feel identified with the dealer, not at all, you're afraid of that murky world of drugs. And suddenly you realize that the assassin's world is equally frightening. Until yesterday you willingly swallowed the arguments his people made to justify their actions. The dealer's world has always repelled you; now you've started to feel repulsion for this other world too.

Even though I was waiting for it to ring, the alarm clock startled me when it did. I stood up immediately and went to the window. I drew a face with my fingers. Droplets appeared around the face in the steamed-up glass. The droplets swelled and became tears that streamed down the glass, undoing my drawing.

I started making the bed, which for me was the least agreeable job of the day. Mom came into the room as I was flattening sheets and straightening pillows. She asked if I'd slept well and gave me a kiss. She held one end of the sheet.

"You'll never learn, lazy girl," she said, smiling happily.

She unmade the entire bed. Blankets and sheets and my pajamas—all went on the floor. She took clean sheets from the wardrobe. We started making the bed the way she likes it: we spread the bottom sheet, tucked it under the mattress and flattened it with our hands until there wasn't a wrinkle in sight; then we did the same with the top sheet, and with the blanket. She removed the pillowcase, and we put a fresh one on. She placed clean pajamas where the pillow had been, and then the pillow on top. To finish it all off, we put the coverlet on.

She never once stopped talking in an incessant flow of pretend naturalness. How was I feeling; it was obvious the pills had done me good, because I looked very relaxed, as though I'd slept well; she was going to have to get me new pajamas for Christmas; and why did I never tidy up my desk?

"You should be at the shop by now, Mom. Go. Don't worry about me, I'm fine," I said. If things had been different I might have added, "I'm not a child," but I didn't want to ruin her mood.

"I've taken the morning off," she said.

She started explaining why she had taken time off work, as if this was the most normal thing in the world: she'd been thinking about it for a long time but kept putting it off; she had a million things to do, something about the deeds to Grandma's house and a notary was one of them. Not a word about her staying for my sake.

She was incapable of just talking, so she picked up my clothes and tidied the room as she offered her explanations, all the while trying to appear completely natural. But there was a sadness in her face that couldn't be explained away by her need to console me. I had left a drawer open and she started putting the things inside it in order, organizing socks by degrees of thickness. I went to her and forced her to turn around and look at me.

"Come on, Mom, confess that you've stayed for my sake," I told her teasingly.

She smiled weakly, half embarrassed, as if I'd caught her lying.

"Yes, for your sake too. I've stayed for you too," and her eyes lit up; it was as if getting the chance to say it relaxed her. "We're going to spend the morning together."

"And what about school? I have to go; I can't not go, not today! Dad said yesterday that it was best if I carried on with my normal life, as if nothing had happened."

Mom picked up the dirty bedclothes and my pajamas from the floor. She held them against her chest. She pursed her lips and finally came out with the cause of her unease: "Dad was right. But things have changed. I have to tell you something you're not going to like."

Everything that had happened the previous evening came back to me vividly, just as if I had heard two shots— *Bang! Bang!*—there and then.

"What's wrong?" I said, narrowing my eyes.

Mom gave me a little push toward the door with the bundle of clothes she was carrying.

"Come with me to the kitchen. I have to show you something."

I have no idea where I got the strength to undertake that journey. I don't know what I imagined during that short trip to the kitchen, what I thought Mom would show me, but as soon as I walk into the kitchen and see the newspaper on the table, I know that the bad news she's about to give me comes from there.

"I would prefer it if you didn't have to see this," she says, pointing at the paper, "but there's nothing we can do now."

Just as she finishes talking, I notice my own frightened face on the cover of the newspaper. I pick it up. It must be in everyone's hands by now.

"No!"

I sat at the table and stared at the picture. I felt strange, uncomfortable, worse than if I were about to play in front of an audience wearing an ugly dress several sizes too big. The whole thing seemed unreal: this isn't happening, I kept telling myself, like a prayer, but the photo stayed there. And so did the dead man. There was no one else.

I still have that newspaper. The smell of ink still clings to it. The black and white photo occupies a fourth of the front page, but the composition is just as striking as its size: I'm standing to the left of the frame, in a close-up, my face turned slightly toward the camera. I look frightened and stare at the camera like an idiot, waiting for the photo to be taken.

It's undeniable that it looks like I'm posing.

Near the bottom of the picture lies the dead man.

It was a common event back then; it's still common nowadays. We're used to it. Some still have the energy to get angry, others gave up a long time ago; most look away. Photographers become used to reporting on news like that—so what. They deal with it the way notaries sign papers, it's routine—so what. The man having his tot of wine will look at images of a dead body and it won't make a difference to him—so what. There are photographers who try to escape routine, who try to tell their public as much as possible. And what novel ways of illustrating old news can they come up with to make the news seem new?

The photographer was probably having thoughts like these when I came across him. Today, I think that if I hadn't been there he might not even have taken any photographs. But since I was young, and a girl to boot, I represented the "freshness of youth" to a primarily male audience. I provided the contrast: with me in it, the photo illustrated the battle between life and death.

There was no doubt that I had provided that photographer with the chance to show his ability to give a tiresome news item a different look; instead of giving them the same old fodder, he'd come up with a fresh perspective. It was obvious that the photographer didn't want to do the routine thing, and it was obvious that he had never considered what might happen to me. Such are the downsides of his profession; or so the director of the newspaper said a few hours later.

11

The letters in the caption under the photograph wriggle and jump, I can't put them together. I rub the tears from my eyes. Bit by bit the letters calm down and I read the caption. My name isn't there. The dead man's is.

Abel Ergoien Landa.

My stomach hurts as if someone had given it a sharp nudge. Twelve hours have passed since the assassination. Why haven't I thought until now that the dead man might have a name? Dad didn't mention the man's name when he came back from watching the news last night, and I didn't ask. We've just referred to him as the dead man or the drug dealer. But now the caption under that damned photograph has given a name to the man I watched die: Abel.

The name makes the dead man more human. Closer.

With the photograph still fresh in my mind, I go to the obituaries page. His is the smallest one. It sits at the bottom of the page, lost under the bigger obituaries, as if embarrassed. My eyes zoom in nevertheless.

Again, Abel.

I had heard the biblical tale of Abel and his brother, but the name made me think of Unamuno's novel, *Abel Sánchez*, and the sentence our ethics teacher had taken from the novel and written on the blackboard: "Why was I born in a land full of hatred?" We discussed the sentence for the length of the class.

I start reading the obituary.

"He died yesterday, aged 36, having received the last rites and blessings of the Holy Catholic Church."

Somehow, saying that he was killed yesterday doesn't look as elegant or straightforward. Saying he died yesterday puts him on a par with the other deceased on the page; with those who died of old age or a heart complaint or in an accident. As far as the church is concerned, the dead man (Abel!) didn't have time to curse or to make a deathbed confession either, but who can tell whether he meant to repent or to wish for a blessing? Society always finds hypocritical ways of dealing with crude facts: a mute man once said a blind man saw a lame man dancing. Euphemisms. Or opaque words, to use the words of Perti, our chemistry teacher: "The most effective lies are opaque: they act like a mirror, they don't let the light through." Once, some graffiti appeared at the school entrance, warning a teacher to watch his back. Perti didn't get on with that teacher, but he nevertheless spoke out against the graffiti before starting the class: "What do you think those words are? A warning? Even you know that's not what it is!" He was quiet for a while, making sure that what he was about to say would sink in.

"The graffiti on that wall is a threat. And its aim is to frighten." He was quiet again; he searched our eyes. "Maybe you think that nothing is going to happen to him. But the thing is, it has already happened. The damage is done; there's no going back." He sat at the edge of the table with his head down, in silence. We realized he was telling us something important, but we didn't understand him very well. We looked at each other in amazement. Suddenly, he looked up: "You admire everything that's dressed up as heroism or thirst for justice. It's normal at your age; it's the way it should be, in fact. But beware of those who try to do good by evil means: lies are more easily swallowed when they are disguised as heroics." By the time we got out of class the graffiti had been removed; no teacher other than Perti mentioned it.

When I saw the dead man, Abel, on the ground, I thought he must be the same age as my dad. Around forty-five. But the obituary said that he was thirty-six. I had thought he looked older, I don't know why. Perhaps because of his dissolute look. But the truth was that he was ten years younger than Dad, and, the obituary said, had a mother and three brothers and sisters. It didn't mention a wife or children.

Better that way, I thought.

"Come on, your coffee's getting cold!"

I've been so engrossed I haven't realized Mom has made me breakfast. Next to the mug there is a round of warm toast with butter and cherry jam. I look at Mom gratefully; for me, there's nothing in this world like cherry jam. During the cherry season Mom makes compote with the fattest cherries she can find in the market and puts it in jars. She opens one every now and then. When she sees how Dad or I gobble it down she says reproachfully, "Have you forgotten how expensive those cherries were?"

I eat the first slice of toast eagerly. Too fast to do such a wonderful delicacy justice. I take my time with the second one. The telephone rings. Mom picks it up. Before long I know it's Dad. She asks if he's spoken to our lawyer yet. I don't know what he answers. A couple of minutes later Mom hands me the receiver: "It's Dad. He wants to talk to you."

After asking me how I feel about the photo in the paper, he suggests we do something astonishing at lunchtime: talk to the director of the newspaper and the photographer.

"You've seen the photo. It's not acceptable to use people like that. We have to do something. We can't pretend nothing's happened." He lowers his voice: "I've called the newspaper but there's no one at the editorial office yet. I'd like you to come with me, but I don't want to pressure you."

I don't know how to react. I wasn't expecting this. To talk to the director of the newspaper! What the hell will that achieve? Exert pressure? What for? Dad's softened tone is in itself a way of exerting pressure on me.

"If that's what you think is best . . ." I leave the sentence unfinished.

I hear him blowing his nose at the end of the line. It's clear that I haven't made things easy for him; he feels uncomfortable because I've left the decision to him.

"Well, I don't really know what's best either," he says in the end. "The first thing is to get an appointment. I'll call you as soon as I know more."

He doesn't give up. He doesn't lose hope that I'll go with him. But I want to forget everything: the assassination, the dead man, the photograph. I want to return to my normal life.

I try to sweet-talk him: "You're not going to call me at school, are you? First the photograph, then your call and on top of that going to the newspaper? No, Dad. You go; what would I say anyway?"

"What are you saying? You can't go to school! Everyone's seen you in the paper. They'll pester you with questions everywhere—down the street, in every corner. It's best if you don't go to school today."

"And what about tomorrow? It'll be exactly the same. I can't hide forever. No, Dad, I think it's best if I go to school."

"Are you sure?" he asks, bewildered. "Mom will talk with the school. It's not a big deal to miss one day. You need to rest. You'll be better off, things will be very difficult for you there, you know."

Rest! Difficult! Oh, Dad, Dad, when will you realize that I'm no longer the girl who believes and accepts and applauds everything you say and do? Rather than helping me, you're trying to get me to do what you want—you've always been good at that. You're just baiting me, that's all; you need me to put pressure on the newspaper director.

Even though I was about to explode, I tried to speak calmly: what was I going to do sitting at home all day; I'd be better off at school; the way to avoid complications was to attach as little importance as possible to the event.

As always when he didn't know what else to say or do, Dad played his desperate card: "Talk to Mom."

"OK, Dad, I'll talk to Mom"—*but I'm going to school, I don't care what you say*, I said to myself.

12

I take my hooded jacket and grab my school bag. Mom takes me to the mirror in the hall. She tidies my hair and clothes. "I'd rather you stayed home," she says, but she doesn't dare contradict me. "But if you're sure."

"Yes, Mom, I'm very sure. It's best if I go to school."

"Go. Go if that's what you want, but many of the people who've seen the photo are going to come up to you and say all sorts of things. Don't pay any attention, just say that it's pure coincidence that you happen to be in that photo, all right? Pure coincidence. You didn't see anything, didn't notice anything."

She speaks very slowly, measuring every word and tone and gesture. She doesn't want to hurt me, but doesn't realize that it's precisely her manner that I find difficult to bear.

But I know it's pointless to say anything so I force a smile and offer my cheek. She kisses me goodbye.

I hear her grumble as I walk down the stairs. I go out to the street. The weather has cleared up, but many puddles nestle on the sides of the road. Ominous-looking clouds in the sky. Water gurgles down the pipes on its trip from the roofs to the drains. The air is denser than yesterday: filled with the old, ripe smells of the sea and fallen leaves. Everything feels damp, sinking.

There's no one outside. No cars, no people. The neighborhood is so quiet it feels deserted. I look back at our house. Mom is watching me from behind the curtains. I start walking fast. When I reach the corner, I see the baker taking three baskets brimming with baguettes from the back of his van. He gives me a good-humored little wave and a smile. He is extremely friendly to me, but doesn't stop what he's doing. I'm sure he has seen the photo. He enters the shop pulling one of the baskets inside with him. He's made me feel important, but hasn't said a thing about the photo in the paper. Maybe he hasn't even seen it. I don't know. In any case, I like it that he's been so nice to me. When people treat you like that it makes you feel loved.

As I walked down the avenue of elms in front of the convent, I saw Perti, my chemistry teacher, coming out of a side street and heading toward me. He was dressed exactly the same as always: a thick gray cardigan with a zipper that ran from the waist to the neck, chinos and a wrecked old pair of chestnut-colored shoes. As usual, he walked with a hunch, like someone condemned to carry too heavy a weight. It would have been impossible for someone who didn't know him to guess that he was a teacher.

He's the last person I wish to see at this precise moment, but he comes up to me and takes me by the elbow.

"You didn't get enough yesterday, then? What, haven't you seen them? Come on, come with me," he says harshly, pointing to the end of the avenue.

Only then do I notice two jeeps and around eight civil guards right in front of us, next to a phone booth, at the crossroads between the highway exit and my school.

Whether we want to or not, we have to pass the checkpoint to get to school. My heart is beating wildly and I feel the urge to turn around and go back home, but Perti's hand is still holding my elbow, pushing me on.

"Well, are you coming?" he says.

We start walking. The civil guards have made three young men stop by the side of the road. One of them has his legs spread wide apart and holds his hands behind his head; facing him, a civil guard carrying a submachine gun frisks him fast and hard. The other two boys stand in front of the phone booth with their faces and hands against the glass.

Perti is angry, and he swears under his breath and moves briskly, staring at the civil guards. "Slimeballs, that's what they are!" When we get to the checkpoint he tilts his head back and looks at me. He hasn't shaved, he's looking rough. His crossed eyes have that silvery hue brought on by excessive drinking. It looks like he's about to ask, "What's this kid doing here?" the way the policeman did last night. But no, what Perti said to me was very different: "I didn't know the guy they killed yesterday, and I don't care about what he was or what he did. What they did to him was fucked up, fucked up! And what they did to you too. You're probably shit scared now, you're going to hear all sorts of things—but ignore them all, don't give a fuck about what anyone says. Believe me, it's not worth it." He coughs; he's hoarse. He's not waiting for an answer; he starts banging on about the civil guards. "Do they think they're going to find the killers here, or what? They're at the other end of the world already! You're just stirring up shit, that's what you're doing!" he snarls at them, so loud that they can hear him. It's lucky they don't speak Basque.

One of the civil guards points the submachine gun at us.

Perti starts coughing—he sounds like he's choking. The guard probably thinks his grunts were part of the coughing. He makes a disdainful gesture and, turning from us, points the submachine gun back at the other three.

I put my hand in my pocket and hold the pack of cigarettes, but I don't dare take it out; it always embarrasses me to smoke in front of adults.

Perti keeps talking even as we reach the checking point, quite loudly and without looking at the guards. "What happened yesterday was barbaric, but it's stupid to put every passer-by in jail. It's like these morons want us to forget what happened last night—ask those three over there." My eyes meet one of the guards' gazes. It occurs to me that he might have seen me in the photo. Or that he might be able to understand the things Perti is saying. But he doesn't say or do anything, so we walk past him.

Perti falls quiet. I don't think he even remembers that I'm by his side. We see many young people on the way to school. I'm uncomfortable. Many of them must be wondering what I'm doing with a teacher, especially Perti.

He was an alcoholic—after his wife died in a car crash he drank from the moment he woke—but he managed to keep up appearances pretty well, at least until lunchtime. He was a good teacher; his classes were the best in the school, even though the drink made him ramble on a bit.

I can't remember his first name; everyone just called him Perti. One Monday morning, rumors ran around the class that Perti had spent the last few hours of the weekend in jail. At some point, at the height of his drunkenness, he had punched a policeman who had come to reprimand him for creating a disturbance. There was a huge stir and the class was in chaos. When he finally managed to get some silence he said he wanted to talk about the word "pertinent," and that he wanted to use his face as an example to illustrate its meaning: "My face is pertinent to my condition: the red lump that is my nose and the scabs on my face could only belong to a diehard boozehound like me." The commotion died down after his confession; no one dared say anything else.

It was quite a sight to watch him write on the blackboard, and his diatribes on contemporary affairs were memorable. He didn't care whether the lesson was supposed to be on atomic mass or Avogadro's number or the periodic table: Perti always used the subject of his lessons as a means to rage against the world. "Lead is a dark, heavy, malleable metal. Kind of like the pedagogical foundations of this institution, in fact." And he would snap his fingers, full of glee, as if he had just made an amazing scientific discovery. "Of all the atoms, hydrogen has the smallest mass; it isn't however, as small as the encephalic mass of the politicians in this country," and he would snap his fingers. What he liked best was to rage against the clergy, though: "You think chemistry is a mystery, but not to the extent that it can turn wine into blood," and he would snap his fingers louder than ever.

We walk together for another three minutes. Suddenly, and without saying goodbye, he walks away from me and, crossing the road, goes into a bar.

I look right and left. I don't think anyone has seen us.

13

It started to rain softly. I put the hood of my jacket up and ran to the bus stop in front of my school. I stood under the shelter. I lit a cigarette and savored the bitterness of the first drag. I spent quite some time there, watching the students on their way to school. Most were in a rush; others, however, stood under the shelter like me, but for a moment only, to catch their breath. They never noticed me and, after a few seconds, rushed out toward the school.

I stayed there until the bell that announced the start of the first class rang. Then I ran to the main entrance and got lost in the crowd. The same daily racket of people running up and down the stairs, swarming up and down the corridors.

My classroom was far from the main entrance. I didn't remove my hood. Mixing with the others, keeping my head down, I had no problem reaching the room without being questioned or hearing stupid remarks.

The usual shouts, cheery hellos, comments on the previous day's TV shows, exchanges of notes, making of plans to go to the harbor party in the evening.

And suddenly, above all the voices, one rings out loud and clear: "Have you seen today's paper?"

I don't hear the answer; I don't know if they're talking about me. What I know is that just to think that they may well be talking about me feels quite nice. The same warm feeling I experienced when the baker waved at me.

I take the hood off and lift my head. Then I realize there is something going on by the door to the classroom; people are looking at something that is pinned up there. I go over.

The front page of the newspaper, with my photo on it.

One of the boys looking at the clipping notices me and looks at me half admiringly, half jokingly. He whistles and shouts loud enough for everyone to hear, "It's like you're a movie star!"

And he cackles dementedly, and the whole class cackles back like an echo, but all I hear is *Bang! Bang!*

The whole class stares at me like I'm some sort of star and they are my fans. Some are complimenting me, others scream, they all talk at the same time. There's an astonishing ruckus going on in the corridor. It's loud enough to deafen the air itself. How did it happen? How did I react when I heard the shots? Did I see the assassin's face? What does it feel like to see your own face in the newspaper?

The boy who said I was like a movie star passes me a pen and paper and asks for an autograph.

He starts cackling again, like a madman; they all start cackling.

Imbecility is infectious.

I'm about to cry. I want to become invisible. I feel an urge to turn around and run away as fast as I can. But I can't, because my legs are incapable of following my mind's command. I'm stunned, staring blankly at the pen and paper in front of me.

"Come on, go for it. You embarrassed? You sure don't look like it in the photo!"

Someone steps in and hits the boy's hand away hard. The pen and paper fly through the air.

"You're worse than children!" shouts the literature teacher at the top of her soprano voice. She pulls the newspaper page from the wall and tears it in shreds. She scrunches it up and gives it to the boy: "In the trash!"

The boy stares at the teacher defiantly. It looks like he isn't going to do it. But in the end he takes the ball of paper, turns around, throws it in the garbage can and walks into the classroom. We all follow him, like a herd of sheep.

I go to my desk, take a tissue out of my bag and dry my eyes. Two girls come up to me, telling me not to take it to heart, that I know what that guy's like. Be understanding. Don't make a big deal out of it.

I don't know what he's like and I don't want to know. You tell me. Or better still, tell him he's an idiot, that he has no heart, tell him anything. Maybe then I'll start understanding something. But please don't pity me; feel sorry for him, because he's not even worth the effort it would take me to slap his face.

I don't say anything.

Away with you, busybodies!

I hear a rustling sound: the teacher, walking down the rows of desks. She reaches the dais, takes off her raincoat and straightens her skirt.

"We've wasted enough time as it is!" she says in a stern voice that is in complete contrast with her doll-like looks. She doesn't even say good morning: "Come on, let's get on with our work!"

I didn't even have the energy to take my books out of the bag. My mouth was completely dry; I was staring into space.

The teacher started distributing photocopies. When she reached my desk she left a page on my table and tapped me encouragingly on the shoulder. I didn't lift my head.

When I felt she had left my side I glanced at the photocopy. By the looks of it, the text was a poem. I've always liked books, especially poetry; I sometimes dreamed of becoming a great poet's muse, like those wonderful Tuscan women in the Middle Ages, Beatrice or Laura. I had other fantasies, of course. I was in love with Iggy Pop, and the mere thought that I could one day accompany him on the piano made me incredibly excited. And for a while I even dreamed of becoming a professional handball player, until my piano teacher made me give up because she said the sport was desensitizing my fingers. But I had a weakness for poetry and for a while I even wrote some. I still have the notebook.

But that morning I didn't care about anything. Even the most exultant poem in the world couldn't have lent beauty to the glum picture that sadness and anger had painted inside me; the laughing faces of my classmates are in the foreground of that picture. Time has faded its colors, but it has not made them disappear. Sometimes people tell me about the eventual ideological turnaround of some of those cackling classmates of mine. But even now I find it extremely difficult to soften the hardness of their faces; it was etched in my mind that day.

14

After she has given us all a copy, the teacher asks us to read the poem. I should join the class and read it too; I should turn my eyes to the text and pick up the pencil. I should underline the things I like and the things I don't understand; I should write down the metaphors. But when I open my notebook I see a sticker in the inside cover. I must have put it there a very long time ago.

I close the notebook, and my eyes. Useless. The image is burnt into my retina more sharply than on the sticker itself: the two syringes crossed out with red paint, the target next to them, the motto *Dealers Against the Wall!* underlining it all.

I'm not in a fit state to be here; I don't know why I came. I knew it would be hard when I made the decision to go to school, but I never expected it to be this hard. The worst of it is that this is only the beginning. If I asked permission to go home after this class they wouldn't deny it to me, but what would I achieve by returning home?

I look out the window, surprised at the light that has suddenly filled the class. It has stopped raining, and the sun, after peeking through the clouds for a while, is taking over the sky. Specks of dust dance in a ray of light.

The literature teacher was a small woman. She always wore her hair very short, and she liked her sentences short and succinct too. We called her *Txikierdi* for that reason. She had a temper like thunder and it was a fearsome spectacle to see anyone contradict her: her neck reddened and the veins in her temples looked like they might explode any minute. She had joined a convent to be a nun, but had left soon after to join a vegetarian commune where she lived for many years until she got a permanent contract at the school. She was around fifty when she taught me, and dressed in a youthful, hippie-like fashion: gypsy dresses, dangly earrings, espadrilles. But it was all designer stuff, expensive trinkets.

She was a good teacher; she gave us many handouts to supplement the textbook. She knew how to motivate her students and I think most of us had more reasons to be happy with *Txikierdi* than not to. She liked to depart from the curriculum and be chummy with the students. In some ways she was similar to Perti, particularly as regards the sharpness of her tongue; but they couldn't stand each other. I couldn't figure out why. Perti never shied away from confrontation, and everything he did followed from the things he said. Maybe that was the reason why they always raised each other's hackles. But these are just conjectures, I don't really know what went on.

In any case, we respected her and she treated us with respect. "Often, commercial success doesn't reflect artistic value," she liked to say. And she would add, emphatically: "Thankfully!" But according to some evil-minded colleagues whom *Txikierdi* couldn't stand, there was a hidden aspect to that honorable principle, and it had nothing to do with aesthetics: while living in the commune she had published a couple of short story collections which had had zero commercial success and received no critical praise. If such colleagues were to be believed, *Txikierdi* had become a teacher because she was a failed author.

She turns from the window and steps onto the dais again. She claps her hands twice. It's her turn. Now, she will read the poem for the whole class a few times. So that we get a better sense of the text—that is what she always says. She clears her throat. We're all waiting. It's not just listening to her read that is a pleasure, it's also watching her do it. She has a fine voice and modulates it well; you never hear her take a breath in the breaks. When she reads them, even the most difficult poems take shape, become understandable.

A little cough. Then she raises her voice and, enunciating carefully, starts:

"And indeed, gods of death, I know it's pointless to pray to you, or to talk about you . . ."

Gods of death! The surprise makes me snap out of my stupor as I realize immediately what the teacher's intention is: she wants to use the poem as a pretext to make us reflect on the assassination. It's obvious, and the whole class is devoting unprecedented attention to her every word. I'm so stupid; why didn't I read the poem!

"Seized and fettered the man, so that he cringes, subdued / when you evil ones down into horrible night have conveyed him / Useless it is to implore, then to be angry with you."

She seems to be in a trance; holding the sheet in one hand but hardly looking at it, as if she knows the text by heart. Her other hand, however, aids her delivery—it seems to be talking as eloquently as the poem itself.

"Am I not quite alone? Yet something kind now must be / close to me from afar, so that I smile as I wonder / how in the midst of my grief I can feel happy and blessed."

When she finishes reading, she writes *Friederich Hölderlin (1770–1843)* on the blackboard. Then she talks to us about the poet, especially about his illness and his tendency to rage against the gods.

"Hölderlin's schizophrenia is key to understanding his poetry and mysticism."

After some brief explanations she returns to the blackboard and writes down some of the words she has just mentioned: schizophrenia, pathos, palingenesis, Hyperion.

"His mysticism was far removed from this world, and from us too; we feel very distant from his mysticism, his language, his poems. Don't read Hölderlin for the mundane. For him life and literature must become one. Literature must go in search of life. Why write or read otherwise? Hölderlin used literature to escape the mundane, the everyday."

What is this about literature going in search of life? Aren't you going to talk to us about the sense of rebellion that's so obvious in the poem, or about the gods of death? Yesterday's assassination, doesn't it deserve even half a word from you? It happened right on your doorstep, do you realize that? Can't you see how stupidly arrogant you're being? Your attitude is even further removed from reality than Hölderlin's poems!

Lost in my ruminations, I disconnected from the teacher's monologue just as Hölderlin had disconnected from life. With my elbows on the desk and my head between my hands, I started going over Schumann's piece in my head in anticipation of my evening piano class.

The sound of the door opening brought me out of myself. I raised my head and saw the vice principal in the doorway, talking in a whisper. He said my name.

15

The vice principal acted as if the literature teacher were invisible. He asked our forgiveness for interrupting the class and didn't even look at *Txikierdi*.

I left the classroom feeling very embarrassed. The vice principal closed the door behind me and signaled the way to his office. He had a short, wide, button nose, and an abundant white beard which tobacco had stained yellow around his mouth, and which didn't do much to disguise his peculiar features. He smiled at me. His teeth were yellow too.

"It won't take long, you'll be able to return to class soon," he said, wanting to seem affable. But the sharpness of his breath betrayed him—his nostrils were becoming wider by the minute. He was barking rather than talking. "Don't worry; everything is going to be OK."

I immediately started worrying; I couldn't figure out what he wanted me for.

I walked by his side all the way to the office. He was strolling leisurely, as if he was in no hurry to get anywhere.

We only exchanged a couple of polite sentences.

The principal was away, and on such occasions the vice principal took over his duties. A few years earlier, finding education too boring, he had become involved in politics. He must have thought he could rule the world. But he lost the elections disastrously and returned to teaching. An old story, and one he should have forgotten soon after it happened, but the experience had burned him out, made him bitter. From what I had heard at home he had never been able to overcome his failure and was continuously quarrelling with everybody. He was always involved in some lawsuit or other, if not with the town hall, then with another teacher or with the Parents' Association. His voice was as rough as his temper.

The corridor seemed never-ending. There was no one around. You could hear the sound of our footsteps: the dry, snappy tap-tap of the vice principal's leather soles, the squeaking noise of my rubber ones. At either side, the doors to the classrooms, perfectly aligned. Every now and then as we passed by them I heard a teacher holding forth, or the students murmuring. The vice principal was walking with his head jutting forward; he had increased his pace now, and his eyes darted left and right; he seemed sure of himself, as if he knew everything was under control.

We're reaching the offices. I follow the vice principal, trying to guess what he might want from me. I'm sure it has something to do with what happened yesterday—but what? Maybe it won't be anything important. It occurs to me that it might be my mother. She's probably called to ask how I'm doing. Or maybe my father called, trying to find an excuse to get me to go to the newspaper with him again. If it's either of those things, I can't understand why he isn't telling me anything. *What's going on?* I want to ask the button-nosed sphinx. It would be a very normal thing to do, but I remain silent. I'm not going to ask him any favors. I'll soon know why he took me out of the class.

We walk past his office and into a meeting room full of tobacco smoke. Two men are standing there. I don't know them. They both lift their eyebrows mechanically when they see us come in.

The vice principal points at the green, fake leather sofa. My eyes are drawn to a little table by the sofa because there's a newspaper on it. With my photo on it.

"These gentlemen would like to ask you a few questions. That's all. They are policemen; but you don't need to worry," he says. "I'm going to stay here with you. Sit down."

The policemen nod as if to confirm his words. Dressed in civilian clothes, they look more like bookies than policemen. "Good morning," they say. "Good morning," I say. They smile; I don't bat an eyelid.

The vice principal takes a pack of cigarettes from the table and, pulling two out, offers them to the policemen. He doesn't offer me any, of course. One of the policemen and the vice principal start to smoke. New smoke joins the old, stale smoke.

The three men are staring at me, perhaps waiting for me to sit down. My face feels very hot, I can't hide my embarrassment, so I sit down on the very edge of the sofa. I feel more than naked, I don't know how to sit, what to do with my hands, how to breathe.

The fake leather makes the room smell like a souk. The cigarette smoke probably adds to the overall effect.

One of the policemen, the smoker, takes the paper from the table. He puts his finger on my photograph.

"You were there when they killed that guy yesterday, weren't you?" he asks, and not even giving me a chance to answer, comes a step closer to me: "Don't worry, it's only a formality. It'll take five minutes. You must tell us what you can remember: the color of the assassin's hair and eyes, his clothes . . . anything. Everything you remember."

He is clearly more senior than his companion. He speaks animatedly, but his eyes are very tired. Like two marbles that have lost their shine. He paces back and forth in front of me with his arms crossed; he's making me nervous. The other policeman takes a small notebook and a pencil from one of his jacket's inner pockets and sits down. His hands are big, his fingers thick; he holds the pencil very gracelessly. He leaves the notebook on his knee and digs into his ear with the little finger of his free hand. For quite a while.

I was confused, shocked; I didn't know what to say or where to look.

"Anything. The smallest thing," repeated the senior policeman.

Words started flowing out of my mouth clumsily. I said I didn't notice the killer; I heard the shots, yes, but didn't see his face; I was so scared I could only look at the man who had been shot at; I saw him fall.

I must not have convinced him because he started asking me again:

"What do you remember about the assassin?"

"I only saw the guy who was killed."

"You saw the dead man fall but you didn't catch a glimpse of his killer?"

His words sounded tired. It was as if he had already lost hope of getting anything else out of me, as if he knew he would hear the same thing over and over.

"I felt him run. But I didn't see him," I answered impatiently.

But the policeman wouldn't let it go.

"If you heard the shots, if you saw the dead man fall, you must have seen the assassin. Come on, sweetheart." I was finding his pretend-gentlemanly attitude and his fake smile more revolting by the minute. "Make an effort, try to remember. Any detail might be able to help us. Any-

thing, even the most meaningless thing. Was there something . . . something that might help us trace the guy who
ran away?"

Everything I remembered had to do with the dead
man. His eyes, wide open, as if shocked by what they were
seeing. Just then a thought made me feel cold all over:
what if Abel was so shocked because he knew his assassin?
What if his killer was an acquaintance, a neighbor, a rela-
tive? What if that was the reason for his surprise?

The mere idea left me incapable of thinking of anything else. The policeman, however, didn't notice anything. He took another step toward me. Our knees were
practically touching.

He opened his mouth. His teeth were stained. He was
trying to sweet-talk me.

He was being rude.

"Tell us about the getaway car—the make, anything.
You want to help us, don't you? Maybe you're afraid.
Maybe you're thinking that you might come to harm if
you talk. I know how you must feel. What will your
friends think and rubbish like that. I understand, don't
think I don't."

He talked to me as if he knew me.

The policeman with the notebook gave me an accusing, sideways glance, as if the fact that he hadn't been able
to write anything about the killer was my fault: "You look
like a nice girl. Why are you being so obstinate?"

The other policeman rubs his eyes—they are red from
the cigarette smoke. Suddenly, and for no reason whatso-
ever, he starts shouting at me:

"Great! You've seen everything except the killer! Do
you really think we're that stupid?" He lights up another
cigarette and looks at the vice principal: "One of these

days we'll all realize we've been swallowed up by a big lie. But by then it'll be too late."

My legs feel more tired than if I'd hiked up and down several mountains. But I fight the desire to cry, my disheartenment, my fear: "I've told you everything I know!"

Then I look straight at the vice principal. My embarrassment and my meekness are gone. I realize that, clearly, I have to dig myself out of this hole: no one will feel pity for me, no one will do anything unless I speak up.

"Have you talked to my parents? Do they know I'm here with you?"

The vice principal knocks on his knees lightly and stands up. The policeman who hasn't taken any notes stands up too. And I do the same.

"It wasn't necessary to talk to your parents; as you've seen this was only a formality," says the senior policeman.

The two policemen and the vice principal exchange pleasantries and compliments and pat each other on the back.

I look at them angrily and leave without a word. The door closes with a dry, wooden sound. It makes me think of a coffin being shut.

The long corridor is ahead of me again. I feel light, as if I had thrown away an item of clothing worn too often. I feel freer.

16

This is only the beginning, there's more to come, my inner voice tells me for the second time that morning.

I didn't feel like going back to class to be stared at by everyone again. I went to the library instead, which was at the other end of the building; I knew it would be empty around that time. The reading room was open, so I went there seeking solitude. It was forbidden to smoke inside the school. I lit up a cigarette.

Standing up to the policemen and putting an end to their questioning had put me in an uneasy mood rather than calm me down as I had hoped. The papers, my schoolmates, the teachers, the police . . . they were all after me without caring about how it affected me. I couldn't control the situation; I was at their mercy. I was a helpless fly trapped in an intricate spider web, unable even to see the threads of which it was made. I had been judged—and condemned. The spider was getting bigger and bigger, and would appear to me now as the photographer, now as the policeman, cackling loudly; trapping me in its web was its only pursuit. And I knew it would appear again, in God knows what shape. It would change apparel, but it would still be judge and jury. It was pointless to protest; no one would heed my screams.

"One day we'll all realize we've been swallowed up by a big lie. But by then it'll be too late," the senior police-man had said to the vice principal. I was a youngster as well as a liar, and the fact that I was young meant it wasn't easy to mold me to the system he was defending; I had to be treated with suspicion. I was young and couldn't be trusted, they both agreed.

The policeman who had questioned me was pursuing a quest against lies, and had no other way of going about it but to push things to their limit—that was his only method. And if in the process he had to walk all over Lady Justice herself he would, no doubt about it. I was young and therefore couldn't be trusted, so they had to be careful with me—at least until it was time to make me listen to reason. Until then, I was nothing but a bothersome fly that needed to be kept under control.

I was nothing, I was the lowest of the low.

The policeman's accusing finger ascribed an unavoidable biological sin to being young. I was young, ergo untrustworthy. *Caveamus, igitur, iuvenes dum sumus:* let us be shrewd while we are young, sang the singer in the café where I used to play the piano, replacing the original's jubilant *gaudeamus*—cheerful—with the wiser *caveamus*. When he sang, my friend appeared younger than he was. In everyday life, however, people thought him older than he really was—partly because of the way he dressed, but also because of the things he said. Whenever anyone asked him about his double personality he would say, always *en petit comité*, "I am a chameleon; like society, I adapt." And he would add, "I just defend my interests, as much in the café as on the streets."

The singer in the café could choose though. I couldn't. Thanks to the variants of mathematical probability—a fluke, in other words—I happened to witness an assassination, and, purely by chance, I did not look at the assassin. So what? No one would believe me; every policeman in the world would have used the same cutting irony the policeman had used with me.

"Wonderful! You've seen everything but the killer!"

They could think whatever they wanted. It wasn't my fault that their faculties of perception and judgment were stunted, like ears plugged with dirty wax.

I just heard the shots.

As for the shooter, yes, I did sense him; I even felt his steps as he passed by me, but I didn't look at him. He was a shadow, that's all. I didn't turn, even when I heard the wheels of the getaway car screeching as if they could burn the air.

What did these bland, white-as-condensed-milk policemen think?

All my attention was on the man who had been shot, but not because of guilt or any feeling akin to guilt. That came later. I couldn't move; my muscles were paralyzed. I was trapped like the fly that has fallen into the spider's web; rooted to the spot, with the man's eyes boring into mine.

If I cared about the accuracy of the paper's obituaries, I would say the following: Abel died in my arms. It might be a bit saccharine—very saccharine!—but it's closer to the truth than saying that he died in the arms of the Holy Church. There are things that are repeated so often—*he died in the arms of the Holy Church; I will never forget you; young people can't be trusted*—that they only seem to be said out of conventional convenience. They are like a mask that hides the truth: what Perti refers to as opaque lies.

Once, when fishing was forbidden for a season, my Dad went trout fishing with his friends. They chose a very remote bend in a river; they thought they were safe there, because you needed to actually get there to see it.

The place was brimming with trout; it was a rocky spot and the water ran high. Just as things were getting good they heard a harsh voice shouting from the cliff above: *"Alto a la guardia civil!"* The civil guards were shouting, so my dad and his friends started scrambling like mad, trying to hide behind rocks and in brambly bushes. Again they heard the voice coming from the cliff: *"Dispara, Antonio, dispara!"* They were instructing someone to shoot, and then my dad and his friends heard explosions, the sounds of gunfire and cursing. Dad says he doesn't know how long he spent hiding, too afraid to even breathe, his heart about to burst out of his chest. When they got back they didn't tell anyone what had happened. After a few months, some people invited my dad and his friends to a meal in a nearby town; I can't remember why. As they were having after-dinner liqueurs, one of the hosts shouted *"Alto a la guardia civil!"* while another, lighting firecrackers, roared *"Dispara, Antonio, dispara!"* That is how they found, amid laughter, that everything that had happened on the day they went fishing had been a joke played on them by their host. When they happen often enough, tragic events instill fear. It was fear that made my father and his friends fall for that silly trick.

Suddenly, I hear the bell that announces the break between classes. I've missed the end of the literature class and the whole math class. It's been more than an hour since the policemen asked for me.

The students pour out of the classes shrieking and yowling, like birds when you hit a tree with a stone. The commotion grows louder and louder and, seeing some of my friends heading toward me, I put my head down. I'm afraid of people's curiosity, their questions. I cross the schoolyard quickly and come out onto the street, looking behind me. I need to calm down; the best thing would be for me to leave the school.

The sky is clear and although it's cold, it isn't windy. The light is good, soft; it doesn't have that gray, cold, metallic sheen. The civil guards are no longer at the crossing. And the phone booth is free. That's as big a relief as not seeing the guards there.

17

As I'm about to open the door to the phone booth I see a boy with a thin face on the other side of the glass, walking toward me. He is a senior. He is very active in many of the school events and our paths have crossed a few times. His features are hard, but he has beautiful eyes. The kind of eyes that know how to seduce. He always wraps a rubber band around his thumb, and he is tensing and slacking it now as he walks. It looks like he might want to use the telephone. I know he wouldn't hear me, but watching him wait for me to finish would make me nervous. I motion for him to go ahead. He gives me a grateful smile, but stands in front of me instead of walking into the phone booth. It's me he wants after all.

He looks right and left. He waits until the two girls who walk past us disappear in the distance. He doesn't want any witnesses to our exchange. I know that attitude of his. He looks behind him, and then at the rubber band between his fingers.

"How's it going, did you get over the shock?" he says in a languid voice. He tenses the rubber band.

I guess he's talking about the killing, so I give him a pitiful smile and say nothing, because I don't know what to say. It's a relief for me to think that he's the only person who has been tactful since I walked into the school today. But the boy doesn't raise his eyes from the rubber band, doesn't see my smile. He releases it and I hear it snap against his fingers. He doesn't move a muscle; it looks like it hasn't hurt him at all.

I don't say anything, so he talks again: "You didn't say anything to the police, did you?"

I lift my eyebrows: I didn't expect that. I feel the heat rise from my cheeks to my forehead. I have to make a supreme effort to hold my anger in check.

"What could I tell them? I didn't see anything."

He looks at me for the first time. Stares me up and down, frowning suspiciously.

"Good. Good. That's what I like to hear. I always thought you were a clever girl," he says mockingly. "You didn't see anything, you don't know anything, you were too scared to notice what was happening."

I start to walk away. He grabs my elbow: "Wait a moment, there's something I want to tell you. I'll leave you alone soon."

Why doesn't he bother asking me if I want to listen to whatever it is he wants to tell me, I think. But he's started already, totally oblivious to my wishes; he's telling me some drug addict's story while he stares at a spot on the ground and plays with the rubber band.

Until he started taking drugs, the boy he spoke about had no equal: he was a brilliant student and a gifted athlete; a born leader. But one day some bastard introduced him to drugs. Quickly and nervously he told me one of those stories about drug addicts that are so common— thieving, ruined family, jail. I had heard many like it, especially at home. But the story I'd heard so often felt new and unique coming from his mouth. It was clear that he was talking about something he had experienced first hand; but even then, I felt very far removed from the drug addict's troubles; I had other worries that were more real to me. I couldn't figure out what he expected from me, but, whatever it was, he had come knocking on the wrong door.

The boy stops talking. Some students walk back to school with sandwiches and cans of Coke they've bought in a nearby bar. He stretches and releases the rubber band and lifts his eyes from the ground. First he looks at the students. Then at me. His eyes have lost their charm; now they are just hard, like the rest of his face. I don't know what the reason for the change is—hatred or pain.

The rubber band snaps again—I've lost count of how many times. The rubber band, the story, and the boy himself are making me nervous. I'm trying to work out a way to get out of this one. How to escape. It's my only thought. But why don't I just leave? Why don't I tell him to get lost? Why am I afraid of him? That is what's wrong with me: I'm afraid of him. That's why I'm still here; it is fear that is making me still and silent.

The students are far away now. The boy stares at the ground again.

"Do you know the 'doghouse' near the Aldalur neighborhood? It's a shambles, about to collapse."

I knew immediately who he was talking about. I was familiar with him because Grandma was always saying how she saw him every morning under the church awning, all skin and bones. Although he had his regulars, he opened the door to all who came to the church, hoping for small change. The boy had described the drug addict's house as a doghouse but it really wasn't much more than an abandoned herder's shack; he lived there with a few dogs. We always avoided the place when we went for a trek on the mountain.

"Yes, I know who you mean. But what does all this have to do with me?"

"I don't know if it has anything to do with you, but it has everything to do with me. He's my brother. I thought you should know."

He stops playing with the rubber band and starts flexing his index finger. He attempts a smile, but I know already that he's actually threatening me.

Even though his voice shakes with emotion when he says the drug addict is his brother, the conversation quickly gets hard again.

"What happened yesterday cannot be changed, and thank God for that, because that son of a bitch deserved what he got," he says disdainfully. Then he adds, in a whisper: "Get it into your head: you better stay quiet."

I look at him harshly. I think of saying, "Thanks for the threat," but he turns and walks away before I can voice my thoughts.

Instead of cursing him aloud, I clench my teeth. I don't know what I'm doing in the midst of this madness. More and more I feel like a helpless fly, can see no way out of the spider web.

The policemen wanted to catch the killer; the thin boy, however, wanted to protect him, because in his view the killer had exacted revenge on the man who had destroyed his brother. I understood that much. But I had seen nothing, so I could neither protect nor denounce the killer.

There was nothing I could do. What they thought of me—the policemen as much as the drug addict's brother—carried more weight than anything I could tell them myself. How to get out of that hole, that's what I needed to figure out, because it seemed that having witnessed the assassination was taking me down a more complicated path than I had envisaged. And as far as I was concerned, the photographer had a lot to answer for—all this was mostly his fault.

I step into the phone booth and ring Dad. The secretary at the office answers. Who's calling, and is the call urgent, she asks. I have no option but to tell her who I am. The secretary's voice softens: "Oh, poor darling, it's you! I've seen you in the paper. What a fright you must have had!" She keeps talking, non-stop. I restrain the urge to swear at her and say that I'm in a hurry. At some point, Dad picks up the phone. He starts asking how I'm feeling, but I interrupt him:

"I want to go to the newspaper."

He sounds worried. What's made me change my mind? I tell him we'll talk when we meet.

I can hardly hear what he's saying, because a big truck rumbles by at that precise moment. I half hear him say that he doesn't want to pressure me. He wants to go through the whole thing again, but I don't feel like it; it would take too long.

"I know all that, Dad. I just want to go, OK?"

He says it won't be an easy encounter; he goes on and on, so I tell him a little lie: "Dad, I don't have any more change. When are you going to pick me up?"

"I'm finishing an important job now, but I'll be free in an hour. I'll need another twenty minutes to get there. Shall we say one o'clock in front of the school?"

How can I tell him that I would prefer it if he left right now and picked me up anywhere but in front of the school? But he'd worry and start thinking bad things. That's all my tormented brain needs right now: my father worrying about me.

I say fine, in front of the school, and hang up.

18

I had more than an hour to kill before meeting Dad. I checked my pockets. No cigarettes left; I had smoked the last one in the reading room. I started walking, leisurely, toward the bar where we bought our sandwiches. There were four boys at a table playing cards, who looked like they weren't in a hurry to return to class. Two girls watched them. One of them was as stiff and thin as a broom, and wore braces. The other was short and chubby, one of those inconspicuous people who are so easy to forget. I knew them, but was only really familiar with the one with the braces because she sometimes hung out with my friends.

They didn't see me come in; they were all focused on the card game. *Thank God for that,* I thought. I went to the cigarette machine and bought a pack. Just as I was about to leave, one of the girls saw me and called my name. They all turned to look. The two girls said goodbye to the boys and came up to me. The boys immediately lost interest and went back to their game.

"It's later than we thought. We'll go with you!" says the girl with the braces.

They are both in their final year, although the chubby one is repeating a year. In any case, they are both older than me. It's the photo in the newspaper that has made them act so chummy. Normally they wouldn't even say hello.

The two girls start walking to the school with me in the middle. They think I'm going there too. It doesn't occur to me to react; I don't feel capable of explaining, so I go along with them. I'll decide what to do when we get there.

I start opening the pack of cigarettes. The girl with the braces offers me one from hers with a friendly smile. She even lights it for me. We hardly know each other. I thank her and smile too.

"How are you doing?" she asks. Some of her words whistle slightly because of the braces. "What a shock, eh?"

"I don't know how I'd react if I were you!" says the chubby one. "I'm sure I'd just faint on the spot!"

"They say they got the wrong guy," says the girl with the braces, as flatly as if she were saying the skies are clearing.

I'm shocked; I haven't even contemplated that possibility for a second. They weren't after Abel! What then? But I don't have time to feel relief or anger or anything else, because the chubby girl answers, "Those guys never get it wrong, silly."

"Well, that's what I've heard. It's true that people were dealing drugs near his bar, but he had nothing to do with it," says the girl with the braces as she raises her hand to greet a girl who's passing by. "They were after someone else, they got it wrong. It wouldn't be the first time."

"I don't think it's that simple. Have you seen the obituary? It doesn't mention his wife and children—doesn't that make you think there's something corrupt going on?" says the chubby one. "It can't be good."

A wife and children! And I thought he was single.

The chubby one keeps talking. She's full of morbid details.

"Apparently he left his town when they got divorced. He's been living alone ever since, and now that he's dead his wife and family want nothing to do with him. It's quite sad, isn't it?"

She's talking to the girl with the braces, not to me, really. She probably thinks I know all this. I've appeared on the front page of the newspaper, of course I must know everything. But I don't know anything. The insanity of it all! All I know is that, whether they got it wrong or not, Abel is dead, and despite that, nothing has really changed, other than inside me. But why am I so worried, why do I care whether the chubby girl is telling the truth and his wife and children have really disowned him? I have enough to deal with in my own head, I don't need to worry about other people.

"How do you know all this?" asks the girl with the braces.

"Well, you know, I've heard people say it. Apparently the family is from Tolosa and when they divorced, this drug dealer came here without a penny or a roof over his head." Even though the girl with the braces has said they got the wrong guy, the chubby one is still saying Abel was a drug dealer. "He came here and the first thing he did was open a bar. He must have had *some* money!"

"Ha!" says the girl with the braces.

The two girls gossip incessantly, they've completely forgotten about me. I don't like them; their views are so simplistic, they are making me feel uncomfortable.

I sigh. *Is there nothing else you can talk about!*

It seems they've heard my thoughts, because they suddenly start talking about tonight's concert, which is part of the port festival. Am I going? I am not.

"Won't your parents let you?"

"No, it isn't that . . ." I murmur, and I don't say anything else.

I don't know if they even heard me. They were already engrossed in another conversation about the band that was playing that evening, about a boy who walked by us, about a t-shirt in a shop window. Jesus, they never ran out of things to prattle about. Maybe it was me who was completely out of sync, but I thought they were stupid—thoroughbred silly cows, both of them.

Then we got to the school entrance.

"Crap! To have to go to class now! And math too! What a joy, I'll have a siesta before my meal," said the chubby girl.

"What do you have to go to?" asked the girl with the braces.

"Perti. But I can't go. I'm meeting my dad."

"Lucky you!" said the chubby one. "You should have heard the sermon he made us listen to today! I guess he must have been talking about yesterday's killing, but we didn't understand a word. I think he'd had a few drinks already. He should keep quiet; all he does is talk nonsense, don't you think?"

I suddenly felt the urge to go to my chemistry class. I couldn't, though; Dad would come to meet me in half an hour.

Looking back on what I've written so far, I'm not so sure about my portrayal of Perti. Maybe I've poured too much admiration into my descriptions of him. The two girls, however, talked disdainfully about him and his classes. Most of the students at my school felt the way they did. It's very difficult to bring someone's personality alive through words, but since that's what I am trying to do, I don't want to give the wrong impression. So I have to say that I didn't much agree with Perti's lifestyle, because I don't like people who wallow in their own misery. But he was the only teacher who carried his ideas and his treatment of the students through to their logical conclusions. He challenged us all the time, so much so that he made us angry—he was very good at that. We reacted to everything he said, protesting that he was clearly trying to provoke us. But the way I see it now, he was the only one who made us confront our budding bourgeois contradictions and showed us what they really were: the fact that we said one thing and did the opposite was the result of our hypocrisy, because we lacked nothing, we had food and shelter. He treated us harshly, it's true, and often told us things he shouldn't have. Once—it was the spring of the year Abel was killed—a bunch of us spent some time spraypainting over the Spanish words on the bilingual road signs. When the police turned up we all ran away, but one of us was caught—he wasn't a good student—and had to spend a few hours in jail. The following day, Perti addressed the boy in front of the whole class: "If only you spent a quarter of the time you spend spraypainting traffic signals learning to write your mother tongue properly!" Most of us decided to stop going to Perti's classes, and even went to the principal's office to complain about him. We wanted his attitude curbed. We wouldn't return to class until he said sorry. And so Perti said sorry to the boy in front of the whole class.

"I've put my foot in it, sorry; I shouldn't have made it personal. People prefer generalizations." And looking at all of us, he said: "If only you spent a quarter of the time you spend spraypainting traffic signals learning to write your mother tongue properly . . . but you know what? I'm not so sure that talking like this, to all of you in general, will do any good; none of you will take it personally."

Many people hated Perti, because they couldn't stand his sharp tongue and the things he said. I didn't hate him, but I didn't feel comfortable listening to his diatribes. For those of us incapable of questioning ourselves they were too bitter a pill to swallow.

19

It was clearing up, the sun was coming through the clouds bit by bit. The wind was changing and the air shone like fine steel. I wanted to touch it.

I went for a walk in the park next to the school, heading down toward the river. The paths and meadows were coated with leaves; everything was wet from the rain of the last few hours, so I couldn't amble at my leisure there, listening to the sound of my footsteps. I left the path that cut through the middle of the park and walked on the main path closest to the road. Most of the trees were elms. Behind them, half hidden, were some old chalets in that baroque French style, with stone fronts and slate roofs.

I wanted to walk without having to worry about anything, so every time I came across people I looked away. After a while, however, I forced myself to look them in the eye. No one noticed me; they didn't recognize me from the newspaper. If the people I passed didn't even look at me I breathed deeply, as if I had just surfaced from a long dive.

I walked and walked until I reached the river. The air felt clean and new; it smelled of salt fish. I lit a cigarette, walked down the mossy steps of the dam and dipped my hand in the water. It wasn't very cold. I moved it back and forth for a while. I have always found it difficult to figure out whether the tide is ebbing or flowing. I took one last drag from the cigarette and threw the butt in the water. It headed toward the sea. The tide was ebbing. I stood there for a long time, watching the cigarette butt drift down the river.

I reached the school entrance at the time I had agreed with my father. I could hear distant classroom noises. Just as I was about to light another cigarette I saw Dad's car coming into the car park. He greeted me with the car lights. I put the pack of cigarettes back in my school bag and some chewing gum in my mouth.

I opened the car door, threw the schoolbag on the back seat and kissed him.

"How was your morning? Have they bothered you much?" he said in a playful tone.

I told him about the policemen's visit. I told him what they asked and what I answered, but didn't give him all the details because I knew he would rage if I did. Despite that, I could see him getting angrier and angrier as I told him the story. He listened to me in complete silence, hands on the wheel and eyes on the road, pursing his lips and concentrating on my every word.

When I finished he let out a furious grunt. "You're not even seventeen yet—they've no right to interrogate you! Why didn't they call me?"

"The vice principal was with us all the time," I said, hoping this would calm him down.

"So what? That shit-for-brains should have called me, instead of trying to be the police's best friend!" He slowed the car down and turned the indicator on, intending to return. I asked him what he was doing. He said he was going to have a word with the vice principal.

"No! Please, Dad. It's already happened now, right? Leave it. I made it clear to them that I didn't see the killer and have nothing to tell them."

"If not today, then tomorrow—the bastard is definitely going to hear from me."

I insisted that I didn't want him to do anything; I didn't want any trouble. The vice principal became intractable when someone antagonized him. He couldn't even bear to look at the children of parents that came to him with complaints. I don't know if my words had any effect, but in the end, after cursing freely under his breath for a while, Dad hit the gas and took the road next to the park I had just walked through. After driving by the river for a few minutes, we crossed the bridge by the hospital and took a winding, rugged road; at either side the pastures and farmed fields multiplied as we left innumerable bends behind.

"Where are we going?" I asked, because I could see that we were getting farther and farther from the newspaper offices.

"For a meal. The editor of the newspaper won't see us until four; there's been another assassination—in Eibar this time. First of all, we're going to eat. At least no one can deny us that right."

I had hardly eaten anything in the last twenty hours, but Dad's throwaway mention of another assassination instantly did away with my hunger. I would have happily smoked a cigarette, though. I started riffling through Dad's tapes to distract myself.

Suddenly, Dad turns his head toward me and says something I didn't expect to hear at all: "This whole thing about going to the conservatoire . . . are you sure you want to live off music?"

No, please, not now! I don't want to talk about it again. He must have brought the subject up now for a reason; he must have been thinking about what I said yesterday and finding ways around it, and I don't have the strength of mind to go against him.

"We'll talk about it some other time," I say and start winding my window down. "Do you mind?"

He tells me to open it. I feel the clean air on my face. The northerly wind has blown away most of the dampness and mist, and the view from the car is completely clear. I throw the chewing gum out of the window.

We're almost at the top of the hill, and very soon we can see the sea behind the corn fields, crags, and trees.

"But . . . if you're so sure that's what you want . . . I don't know, but we're going to have to think about it."

It seems to me his voice gets sadder when he says this, as if resigning himself to accept some unfavorable ruling.

When he was in the third year of his architecture degree, he forgot to request that his military service be delayed. So he had to go to the military camp in Ferrol. He was away from his studies for two years. When he returned he didn't have the stamina to return to his degree, but thanks to the influence of some friends got a job as a draftsman in an architect's office, which he held for the rest of his life. Even though he hadn't finished his degree he liked to pretend to people that he was an architect, despite my mother's reproachful looks or people's mockery. Still, everybody loved him, because his fantasies didn't harm anyone. I've always thought that he adopted this buffoonish act to get over the disappointment of not having finished his degree.

"Really, Dad. I shouldn't have brought up the subject yesterday. We'll talk about it some other time. Not today. There's no hurry," I say without a trace of anger.

"OK, then we won't talk about that, but you'll let me turn on the radio, won't you?"

He turns the radio on; he probably wants to hear the news about the assassination. But I tell him I don't want to hear the news, and hand him a tape without checking to see what it is.

Boleros.

"It might not be as good as the music you play, but tone-deaf people like me are also entitled to listen to music," he says, smiling.

He was a very special person, Dad, and funny too; he was very good at telling stories. He had such an imaginative way with words that the simplest anecdote could be made to sound as dangerous as any Dick Turpin adventure, or as sensual as one of Casanova's encounters. Sometimes he ended up believing the things he said, just because he had said them so often. It was nice to be around him because he never lost his good humor, and if he did, his bad mood didn't last long. "So what, I don't have a right to get angry?" he'd say. For Dad, negativity and depression were the worst things in the world. He couldn't stand pessimists like my boyfriend—the type of person who, despite having every reason to be happy to be alive, expects something bad to happen at every turn of their lives. Dad was very unhappy when I moved in with him, but never told me anything until we broke up. "You know what?" he said then, "You're suffering now, but believe me, your life will be better for this."

I have many memories and images of my father, but they don't form a coherent whole. I see them as photographs in an album, not as a film with a beginning and end. He dreamed of the day when he could retire and dedicate all his time to what he loved most: fishing. He died six months ago—two years before he was due to retire—of intestinal cancer.

I often think that I didn't really know him, that I saw only the surface—that I was never able to see his different sides. Maybe in a way I am writing to fill this lack too. In any case, memories are not the only thing left to you when someone you love dies; apart from becoming softer and learning from the pain, you feel the need to offer the love you didn't give to that person to someone else. Perhaps that is why I now get on better with my mother than I ever did.

20

After we reached the top of the hill, the road zigzagged endlessly downward. We could see the blue sea and a few white clouds right in front of us. The wind was northerly and the sun glinted on the foamy waves, giving them a steely sheen.

There were almost no cars on the road, but every time one appeared Dad had to stay very close to the verge because of the narrowness of the road and the poor visibility. He didn't talk; he was concentrating on driving. I changed the boleros tape for a jazz one. *How deep is the ocean*, Billie Holiday sang. Oscar Peterson played the piano.

"Remember you're tone-deaf and don't like jazz, don't lose your concentration!" I teased him.

After a few minutes he points at a chalet perched on the top of the cliff.

"That's the restaurant, we're here."

The parking lot is full. Most of the cars are expensive. Dad finds a space in front of a hydrangea bush. We get out of the car. The sunshine is wonderful, but the wind is still very sharp.

The entrance to the restaurant faces the sea and we practically have to walk around the building to get in. We can feel the waves crashing against the rocks. The cliff is a few yards ahead of us, and Dad wants to take me to the top, to a small vantage point with an iron railing, but I tell him I don't want to, that it scares me. We go into the restaurant. There is a huge bay window with stone steps to the right and left of it. On the glass panes, clouds fly fast above the turquoise sea.

The restaurant is full of people, but Dad had the forethought of booking a table. Everything is luxurious. It's clear that he wants to spoil me.

"Do you like it? It's nice, isn't it?"

I agree with him. I almost ask him "Do you?" remembering what Mom often tells him: "You're brilliant at making people believe you're rewarding them when in fact you're just pleasing yourself."

The maitre d' comes over very solicitously and shakes our hand. First Dad's and then mine. His voice is slightly nasal. He talks to Dad, doesn't even look at me. On a normal day this would annoy me, but today it's a relief. He asks for Dad's jacket, and waits for me to hand over my coat, but I tell him it's OK, that I prefer to keep it with me. He hands Dad's jacket over to a girl with very sparkling eyes.

With the maitre d' leading the way, we walk through the restaurant. A very strong smell fills the air. It isn't food, though: there are all sorts of flowers everywhere, mostly lilies, with their white, fragrant petals—it is them I smell. He takes us to the tables in front of the bay window and points ceremoniously at a small one.

The sun shines fully on the table and makes Dad's eyes crinkle. The maitre d' asks if we'd like him to pull the blind down. Dad says no, we prefer it like this.

We sit down. The chair is quite high and my legs don't quite reach the floor. I pull my trousers up to be more comfortable. I suddenly think of the concert dress and laugh inwardly; I imagine Dad's reaction if I told him I had tried the dress on.

But Dad's attention is on the wine; he is sniffing the glass the sommelier has poured for him. He lifts it up, looks at it against the light. He takes a little sip. He swirls it in his mouth. Then he swallows it and signals his approval to the sommelier—with more affectation than the most professional wine taster in the world.

I can't remember what we ate. The dishes themselves were as sophisticated as their names. Dad was talking freely, seeking my involvement. I humored him, laughed at his innocent jokes at Mom's expense, at his funny descriptions of things that had happened to him with his friends or at work.

It was too nice, and it didn't last long.

Two men walk into the restaurant making a lot of noise, not caring much about whether they are bothering the rest of us. When they pass by our table, one of them stops to stare at me, trying to remember where he has seen me before. He's wearing a dark green baseball cap. I feel I have been found out, as if I were naked; I don't know what to do, where to look. The few seconds he spends staring at me feel like an eternity. I'm afraid he might try to talk to me, but in the end he moves on to a table behind us. His companion is already seated there. The man who has been looking at me is going to eat with his baseball cap on.

How crass!

Dad has noticed everything and unlike me has probably found both the scene and the man funny.

"What a weird guy! He must have seen you in the paper. Fame has its good and bad sides," he says, lowering his voice and laughing softly, not wanting the men at the other table to hear.

I don't find his comment funny, and I let him know. He gets nervous; it's obvious that my words have offended him. He starts to apologize and challenge me at the same time: it was a joke, sorry about that, but I shouldn't take it like that.

"And how should I take it, do you think?"

"Not so seriously."

"Not so seriously? You're lucky it's not you in that photograph!"

"Fine, so that man has probably seen your photo this morning, but he hasn't seen you before." And sounding as grave as if this was something he had been studying his entire life he tells me: "When we look at images in the media we only recognize the faces of people we already know or those who appear in them often."

His wisdom doesn't offer much consolation.

"Please, Dad. Let's leave it. I don't want to talk about it anymore."

They brought us the appetizers. Dad was trying to get us back into an easygoing mood, and talking in the same jokey tone about his student life, before he married Mom: the parties, the girls, the pranks they played on their teachers. I knew he was trying to entertain me, but I couldn't take it in the same spirit as before. So I feigned interest. Suddenly he started chuckling and telling me the story I had heard him tell so often before, about the time they went fishing. "*Dispara, Antonio, dispara!*" I gave him a baleful look. I didn't need to tell him it wasn't the best story to tell at the present time; he immediately realized he had put his foot in it. He said sorry and fell quiet.

Dad wasn't very good at dealing with uncomfortable situations. Silence made him nervous. Deep down he couldn't cope with not being given attention. I think he was afraid of solitude; that's why he always had to play the buffoon.

We've finished our meal and are waiting for desserts. Dad has been uncomfortable since he tried to tell the anecdote about the civil guards; we've hardly spoken since. We still haven't even mentioned the visit to the newspaper. I'd like to know how we're going to go about it: what we're going there for, what I should say.

He must have read my mind, because he mentions it before me:

"Our lawyer says he'll look into the possibility of suing the newspaper for publishing the photo, but I don't know, it's not that simple." He pauses and looks me straight in the eye: "I'd like to know what you think. In the end, it's you they're going to bother most of all."

Suing, lawyer . . . I don't know what it is about those words, but they make me uneasy. I can hardly concentrate on what Dad is saying. Not even twenty-four hours have passed since the killing, and it feels like a year.

"No!" I say, louder than I intended.

The two men at the table next to ours look up. The man with the green baseball cap lifts the visor with his hand as if to greet us. Then he says something to his companion. It crosses my mind that he must have remembered where he has seen me. I feel embarrassed and turn my head toward the bay window. Reflected in the glass panes, the two men are still talking about me.

I remember that I stood up and went to the toilet. I turned on the tap, gathered water in my hands and splashed it on my face again and again. My willingness to go to the newspaper was waning fast; I didn't feel like it at all. I dried my face. I would tell Dad he could go alone.

When I returned to the dining room the two men sitting at the next table were engrossed in a discussion about a building's blueprint they had spread on their table. They didn't even look at me.

It looked like Dad hadn't even noticed my distress, because he picked up the conversation where we had left off.

"You're right, we won't sue them. Who knows how long the trial will take—that's not what we want. But we can't let it pass and pretend that nothing has happened," he lifts his head looking for a waiter. "We have to get going, otherwise we'll be late."

Dad lifts his hand to get the maitre d's attention. "Psst!" he says, just like the photographer said to me yesterday.

Suddenly it seems a matter of life or death that I speak to that photographer. Dad is right: he doesn't deserve to get away with it, as if he had done nothing wrong. He'll have to look at me in the face, and I'll look at him too: *You're nothing without your camera, are you? What gives you the right to mess up someone's life like this?*

We pay the bill and get up to leave. I pass by the table where the two men are sitting with my head held high. The man in the baseball cap lifts his eyes from the blueprint.

Despite that, my head stays up.

21

I've forgotten what most of the office looked like, but I remember the big painting in the newspaper's waiting room very well. The portrait of the notary who had founded the newspaper filled most of one wall. He had a narrow face, one of those thin, scraggly, tobacco-stained moustaches and the somber look of someone with solid opinions. Whoever had hung that painting of no artistic value in that room had intended to intimidate the visitors. But the portrait didn't transmit anything other than power: no zest, no passion; not a trace of humanity. Nothing. Everything about the portrait and the man it depicted lacked substance. Even if the first impression was intimidating, you only had to look at it twice to realize that everything in that painting—the use of color, for example—was weak.

We had to wait for a long time for the editor to receive us. Almost half an hour after we arrived, a stick of a girl wearing a red miniskirt came to take us to an office decorated in a style that was intended to be elegant but smacked of nouvelle riche taste. Every time I remember that room I think that only someone who was very vain and proud of himself would be able to work in a room like that.

The editor was on the phone; he signaled to us to sit down. We each sat in a deep leather armchair. The girl asked if we wanted anything to drink. We said we didn't. The girl left.

It was incredibly hot in the office. The massive windows in front of us were half steamed up, and the shapes of the roofs and the buildings they gave on to were distorted.

Finally the editor hangs up the phone. He leaves his desk and comes toward us. He is holding a crumpled white handkerchief. His suit is the color of egg yolk; he carries a fountain pen and a pencil in his breast pocket; his silk tie shimmers; he wears brown English shoes. His elegance is not matched by his physique, however: excess food and drink and a life free of physical exertion have left him with a belly that protrudes massively above his belt.

He passes the handkerchief from one hand to the other to shake our hands. He greets us in clumsy Basque, then shifts to Spanish: "Sorry about the wait. The assassination earlier today has forced us to change our schedule, that's what's delayed me. They've arrested three young men, but they haven't confirmed that they have anything to do with the assassination," he talks quickly, stumbling from one thing to the next. "Do you know it's almost certain now that yesterday's killing was a mistake? We've managed to speak to the man they were looking for. He hasn't caught his breath yet."

I don't know if I should be happy or sad to hear that Abel's assassination was a mistake. Judging from the editor's words, only Abel's killing is a "mistake." The one that took place today somehow isn't. Suddenly, it crosses my mind that a newspaper must be the perfect place for Perti's opaque lies: here they can be soaked up in ink and presented to the readers in all their shining glory.

The editor continues: "I hope we have a chance to talk in peace for a while. I've asked my secretary to hold all my calls." He looks at me and smiles unconvincingly. "So you're the girl we've made so unhappy. You will understand that in a business like ours it's difficult to control everything. Having to bring out a newspaper every day is no joking matter."

I try not to get nervous: I don't look down, I don't smile back, I keep my legs crossed.

The editor flattens the handkerchief out a bit and pats the sweat on his forehead dry. Then he crumples it again and hides it in his fist. He keeps prattling non-stop; I think it's his way of dealing with delicate situations and covering up uncomfortable silences. He hardly even looks at my father.

Unexpectedly, Dad interrupts him in the middle of a sentence: "We'd like the photographer to be here too."

The editor lets out a nervous sigh. Yes, he understands. He goes to his desk and hits the intercom button—so hard that it sticks. He whispers something into it and then releases it again with the help of a nail. He sighs again. He returns to us. He says he's sorry, but we won't be able to speak to the photographer.

"I thought he was here—but I'm sorry, he isn't," he says. "He went to Eibar earlier to take photographs of the assassination and isn't back yet."

He starts to give us a jumbled, breathless exoneration of the photographer's actions without pausing to hear our retort. Suddenly, he stops to pat his forehead dry again, and his eyes shift from the handkerchief to me.

"He didn't mean any harm, my dear, he's a professional through and through."

I thought Dad would lose his temper, but instead he spoke very slowly, pronouncing his words very clearly:

"Someone who acts so carelessly toward people cannot be a professional through and through."

Often afterward, in many long discussions we had, Dad would start retelling Mom and me this story using this particular sentence. He was proud of it and wanted us to remember that moment.

The editor was silent for a while; he didn't know what to say. The normal thing would have been for him to use the photographer as a scapegoat and blame it all on him—Dad confessed to me later in the car that he had expected that—but instead he started theorizing, perhaps thinking that practical responsibility could blur the usual notions of right and wrong.

"Each event, even the most apparently unimportant one, is a world, and many different pieces make up that world we refer to as an event. All we can do is describe how that happens, that's our job."

The editor was nervous. It was obvious that all he could think about was how to get rid of us. He didn't know where to look or what to do with his hands.

Dad, however, didn't lose his cool or his presence of mind. "Your photographer yesterday did something other than describing an event; he used the fear of a girl who didn't know how to react. And that's called mendacity—and note that I chose not to use a stronger word here."

"That's your opinion, and I won't get into whether or not it is mendacity. But the public has a right to information. Our sensibility demands that we protect private interests, of course, we're not made of stone; but not to the point where we put private interest before public interest."

I had found it difficult to follow their conversation since the editor had said the photographer was in Eibar. I'm just retelling what Dad repeated to us so often afterward, although I'm not reflecting the fierceness of the argument. What I remember—as clearly as if it had happened today—is that I had a question for the editor on the tip of my tongue, and the question was whether he knew of any good recipes for making jam. I don't know why I thought of such a stupid thing. Maybe because of the peachy downiness of his face.

Something Dad said then made my ears prick up again: "And you really think that if my daughter hadn't appeared in that photograph the public interest you mention wouldn't have been served?"

"No, you're right, public interest would have been served without it too, of course. But today's newspaper, thanks to the dexterity of our photographer, provides complete information. I would say, even, that it provides information that's full of ethical content."

Dad punched the arm of his armchair.

"Full of ethical content? What a way to twist words! You call the desire to sell more newspapers ethical? If keeping quiet about an event brought you personal or political gain I'm sure you wouldn't publish it."

The editor could hardly disguise his fury.

"You're wrong. What this newspaper did yesterday has nothing to do with what you say. We contrasted a girl's innocence with a repugnant crime, can't you understand? We illustrated the struggle between good and evil all of us here are living with daily, and I think we illustrated it to perfection."

It looked like he was about to add something, but he didn't say any more. All he needed to do was ask whether we were on his side in that struggle.

Dad was on the brink of saying something offensive. He breathed deeply.

"I am an architect, and one single mistake on my part can cause a house to collapse, you don't need to be a genius to know that," he retorted. "But you journalists, do you realize the number of things your mistakes cause to collapse, how much damage you can do with the excuse of fighting evil? You have a lot of authority, you dictate what people should think, no one controls you, and if you damage someone on your way it counts for nothing. Or if it does count, it's taken as due sacrifice at the altar of the fight against evil, unavoidable collateral damage, that's all. And yesterday it happened to be my daughter's turn to be that sacrificial victim."

The editor ran out of patience and stood up. The photographer hadn't done anything against the law, the newspaper hadn't broken any laws. If we wanted to go to court, that was our right, but we would only be wasting money.

Dad stood up too—and so did I, after him.

"We only came looking for some human decency, nothing else," he pointed at me.

"You haven't apologized to her at all; you haven't even said you're sorry. You say the law is on your side, and maybe that's true. But you know what? Maybe the law does protect you, but the laws of human behavior don't."

Dad signaled for me to go to the door, and I went out before him. I think I heard the editor say a cheerless good-bye, but I'm not sure.

And then, who do I see at the entrance of the news-paper office but the boy I saw in the moving van. He's drinking a cup of coffee and talking animatedly with the doorman. He hasn't seen me. He throws the paper cup in the bin, says goodbye to his friend and walks toward the editorial office. He doesn't see me until he is next to me. He stops dead in his tracks, looking serious and sad. He says "Hi" and reddens. He is nervous, but doesn't seem surprised.

"I saw you in the paper today," he says with a shy smile.

I wait for him to complete the sentence, I think he must be about to say something else: *What a shock, eh? Have they hassled you much? What a shitty thing to happen to you?*

I don't know what, but I'm sure he must be about to say something. But he doesn't. Well, he does—he says he's doing some work experience at the newspaper. He smiles broadly at me and looks a bit proud. I can see that he's happy to be working at a newspaper.

He says he's running late, and heads for the editorial office.

When I saw him yesterday he was going to the scene to find out about the assassination.

Saddened, I watch him go. When he passes the waiting room, he looks up at the portrait of the founder of the newspaper.

22

Dad was telling Mom about our visit to the newspaper's office. I was putting scores in my school bag. She was watching my every move. I knew she didn't think it was normal that I wanted to go to the music academy, but she didn't dare say anything. Dad continued to rage against the newspaper editor. I zipped up my bag. Mom came over to me very softly and helped me put on the bag. She told me to come home straight after the piano lesson, nothing else.

I took the beach route. The pavement was covered with a fine carpet of sand that the gale winds had blown in. Every so often a wave would hit the seawall with a tremendous slam. I remembered the cigarette butt I had thrown into the river that morning. *Idiot!* I said to the sea. It was something I had done since I was a kid: call the sea names when I felt low. *Dimwit! Blockhead! Flea-brain!* Most of them I had learned from my grandfather. Back then I didn't know what many of them meant, but I knew that a child wasn't supposed to use them and, full of the thrill of breaking rules, pronounced the words with even more gusto, even if it was only in my head. No one heard me but inside I was shouting: *Chicken! Weakling! Sissy!* And it seemed to me that the waves answered with more and more resentment, and grew taller and fatter and prouder as they cleared the surface of the sea and reached for the sky. I was sure that the waves were responding to me, that they were angry with me, but instead of getting frightened, this emboldened me. *Sellout! Bonehead! Imbecile!* I was mightier than the sea.

This morning's cigarette butt, however, was already nothing. And me? Was I any better than it?

The biggest wave so far slammed against the seawall. By a miracle I didn't get drenched. A flock of seagulls flew above me making an awful, deafening din. I think they were laughing at me. When the seagulls flew away I stopped cursing the sea and started walking again.

The sun was low and its light only reached the promenade through the alleys between buildings, creating stripes of light and shade, cold and warmth.

I reached a street parallel to the place where the killing had taken place; I was walking on the side facing the sea, not the buildings. I considered for a moment whether I should go that way—it was the shortest way to the academy. Part of me wanted to know how I would react to seeing the place without the body there. Another part of me scolded myself for morbidly wanting to upset myself, for being so childish.

I walked another hundred yards or so, past a hotel, then turned right into the streets. It was worse than walking by the crime scene. There was a half-abandoned plot of land between the hotel and the main street, with a crumbling hut in a corner. It was full of rubbish and old, broken things: rusty cans, fragments of roof tiles, car tires, wrecked tools—all sorts of junk. The plot had been like that for a long time, nothing was built there; the owners couldn't agree, there was some dispute regarding an inheritance. It stank unbearably of piss when the sun shone on the hut.

It's used by drug addicts. There's some faded graffiti on the old, crumbling brick wall that half-heartedly fences off the plot; it's the same motif as the one on the sticker in my notebook: two syringes crossed out with red paint. The target next to them. The motto *Dealers Against the Wall!* in red.

Something in the pile of rubbish makes a noise—God knows what's in there. What am I doing here—taking pleasure in self-punishment? I run away almost desperately, and arrive at the academy out of breath. As I walk up the stairs, I hear the soothing, well-known sounds of singing lessons, a teacher shouting for attention, fingering exercises and *arpeggios* on a piano.

My piano teacher opens the door, gives me a loving smile, and says, with her voice full of the pride a teacher feels toward a gifted student: "But, darling, what are you doing here?"

She says she's seen my photo in the newspaper, that it must have been terrible for me. There's been another assassination and they have arrested some young people; there's going to be a demonstration and everyone is feeling very edgy. She hadn't expected me, but she's very happy I decided to come.

Her tone, her dress, her hairstyle . . . she's from a different age. Her attempt at youthful make-up doesn't do much to conceal this.

I sit in front of the piano and start doing exercises to warm up my fingers. I'm all fired up, and do some fingering, some *arpeggios* and some *glissandos*, following them up with some easy pieces, one after another, without pausing. I'm in good form.

"Do you remember what Schumann said to Clara Wieck about the pieces from *Scénes d'enfants?*" she asks, but without pausing to hear my answer, she squeezes my shoulders gently and repeats a sentence I have heard from her lips very often: "'These little pieces are sweet: tender, like life; full of hope, like the future.' Are you ready?"

I nod.

"Go on then! The first *scène*!" she says, encouragingly.

I start to play *Hommes et pays lointains*. My teacher doesn't miss a note; as always, she listens with every fiber of her body. I finish the first *scène* without any serious mistakes; I have internalized it pretty well, because it's the first one. She comments on a few adjustments that I should make in the seventh bar, but turns the page of the score. That means she thinks I've done good work. Then I play *Historie bizarre*. No problems there either. Following my teacher's advice, I play *Colin-maillard* like a game of hide and seek; I'm dying to reach the fifth *scène*. *Bonheur parfait*, and I make three mistakes in the fourth one. Annoyed at myself, I play *Désir d'enfant* again, this time without mistakes.

My teacher smiles: "Show me now. Come on, go easy."

I sigh. Abel and the photographer come to my mind at the same time. My hands are drenched in cold sweat. I'm afraid. Maybe I can't do it. I run my hands down my trousers to get rid of the sweat and the tension. I clench my fists and spread my fingers wide, over and over again. I spend quite some time just doing that.

"I understand; you haven't had the peace of mind to work on the adjustments I told you about yesterday, it's OK."

How can I tell her that I played it brilliantly yesterday, precisely that piece? She wouldn't believe me, and besides, I'm not going to play it well now—I'm convinced I won't be able to play it the way I did yesterday.

I start the metronome and prepare to play *Bonheur parfait*. My teacher starts the chronometer on her wrist. The first three bars come out too loud, and I stop. She doesn't say anything. I breathe deeply. If I was able to do it yesterday, why not today?

I clench my teeth and start again.

I play the first few bars exactly on the beat and with perfect emphasis; I play without mistakes for the first thirty seconds. My playing is completely synchronized with the metronome. But I can hear my inner voice panicking, telling me that the moment for the change of tone is about to arrive—*Almost there! Now, right now!*—and my heart starts beating faster and louder than the metronome. I can't hear anything else: the moment of truth has arrived. And, as if of its own accord, without losing vigor, the right hand gives prominence to the left. The two hands are in conversation, and I am reaching the last few seconds of the piece. It seems to me that hours have passed. The last bar, the last chord. It's over.

My teacher stops the chronometer and places it in front of my eyes: "One minute and eight seconds!" she says, full of amazement. "And without mistakes!"

I play *Bonheur parfait* twice more, and except for a couple of small things, I make no mistakes.

"At last! It looks like you have it. You're doing well. In the next few days you need to work on the seventh *scène*. Do you know what it's called?" she asks, smiling as she turns the page of the score: "*Grand evénement*. The same as what today's lesson has been for me: quite an event."

23

Precise, sonorous death tolls filled the air as I left the academy. Then the bells rang the time. For as long as they lasted it felt like there was no other sound in the world. When they ceased, however, it seemed to me that the usual clatter and hum of daily life was louder than ever.

I headed home, but unlike the previous day I took the path by the station. The red light of dusk illuminated everything, and it wasn't cold. Perfect walking conditions.

I felt light and happy after playing *Bonheur parfait* without mistakes. Abel's killing, the profound impact it had on me, all the disagreeable experiences I had as a consequence—everything seemed to be moving further and further away from me. Time would pass and I would forget. *It's fine, really,* I thought, *I have to stop these miserable thoughts, I have to unload all these bleak memories, I can't spend my entire life poring over one event. Bye, Abel. It's hard, I know, but I have to say goodbye. I have to live.*

I saw two policemen standing on a street corner near the church. They kept looking right and left, as if they were waiting for something to happen. I passed them without a second thought. I wasn't going to be embarrassed. I reached the square by the church and saw another two policemen on the other side of the road, half hidden amongst the vegetation of a nearby garden. I looked at them too; I wasn't worried. I didn't know what they were doing there, and I wasn't interested.

All the bars and shops in the neighborhood were closing, and there were no lights in the windows of nearby buildings. There was none of the usual bustle and noise and hardly any traffic. Everything was out of the ordinary, but I was too involved in my own happiness to realize the strangeness of the situation.

Just then, a long black car stops in front of the iron gates by the entrance to the church. There's a coffin inside the car. Hanging from the back door, a wreath wrapped in a red ribbon with gold lettering that reads Your Parents. Only that wreath, nothing else. After a few seconds another car arrives and parks near the hearse. It's a small red car. An old man gets out, dressed in black, and after him, a woman, equally old and also dressed in black. The woman holds the man's arm. They walk slowly; it's difficult to tell who is supporting whom.

It occurs to me that they must be Abel's parents.

A few other people I hadn't noticed until then emerge from the shadows near the church. They look like ghosts drawn out by the light; the way they look right and left and take small steps makes them seem hesitant, uncomfortable; as if they are afraid someone will bother them. They approach the couple. They offer their condolences: they embrace and kiss them; they shake their hands and pat their backs.

I don't know any of them.

The funeral director, who is wearing a gray coat, opens the back of the hearse and takes out a collapsible metal trolley. The men look at each other. They are uncomfortable and don't seem to know what to do. A priest comes over, dressed in his mass regalia. He makes the sign of the cross. Everyone standing near the hearse does the same. Unconcerned, the funeral director pulls at the coffin and drags it on top of the trolley. He pushes it away from the hearse and steps back. Then I see, on the back of the coffin, the golden initials A. E. L.

I associated those golden initials with a disagreeable memory from my childhood; I still don't know why. I loved merry-go-rounds as a child, and perhaps it was the golden colors in them that made me associate the two things. I don't know. In any case, what I liked best about the merry-go-round wasn't going around it exactly, but rather the fact that Dad would be standing in the exact same spot every time I went around on my horse. One turn and Dad would be there, another one and Dad would still be there, waving his hand and smiling at me. Once, during one of the turns, Dad wasn't there. The merry-go-round kept turning. No sign of Dad. I tried to release the safety chain, but couldn't, and the merry-go-round kept turning and turning. I was crying and hiccupping inconsolably when I saw Dad again, carrying an ice cream cone in each hand. He gave me one when I got off my horse. I threw it on the ground.

The priest starts walking to the church very slowly. The funeral director gestures for the men closest to him to take hold of the coffin. Just as he is about to begin pushing the trolley himself, four men come near him with their heads hanging low; they lift the coffin to their shoulders and walk to the church. Linking arms, the elderly couple follows the coffin. The rest follow them. There must be about thirty people, no more.

The funeral procession walks through the gates that prevent the drug addicts from sleeping under the church awning; step by mournful step, in silence.

After a couple of minutes they all stop in front of the main entrance of the church. The priest starts a prayer before they cross the threshold. They all cross themselves. Just then, I see a lanky and fashionably dressed young man approach the policemen. He has a cigarette butt between his lips. It's the photographer again! My heart skips a beat. He asks the policemen something, and they point at the church. The photographer looks annoyed and throws the butt on the ground. I think he's angry because he's too late.

He crosses the road in three small jumps, shaking his head all the while. He feeds a new film into the camera as he walks. He starts taking photographs as soon as he reaches the spot where the funeral procession has stopped. He stands in one place and his flash illuminates the scene. Then, from another angle, continues taking photographs and lighting up the entrance of the church until they all get inside. He looks at his watch and writes something down in a notebook. He turns and leaves as suddenly as he arrived.

A shiver of fear runs all the way down my spine. There's no air left in my lungs; my whole body is locked in a painful spasm. I'm as paralyzed as if a knife had been put to my throat: even if I wanted to scream or cry I wouldn't be able to. I'm trapped in a nightmare; that is what's happening to me. I'll be fine when I wake up; only then, if ever, will my perfect happiness start.

All these thoughts crowd my head, and I have to rub my eyes, because I see Perti walking past me with an uneasy step but with his head held high. He's in a world of his own and doesn't see me. Just as he's about to cross the road, he stops as if suddenly remembering something he had forgotten. He looks back, first at the closing shops, then at the darkened windows and balconies. He looks like someone who is looking for a fight, as if he's about to start shouting: *Hey you, cowards hiding behind the net curtains! What are you afraid of? Can't you see the man is dead? The poor wretch can't do anything to you now!* But he lowers his head and sees me. Even though his eyes are shining he looks sad; he doesn't seem very drunk.

I look at him like a bird about to be shot. He snarls bitterly at me:

"What the hell are you doing here? Go home!"

I'd like to tell him that my knees can barely hold me; that I'm incapable of walking. But I stand there, silent and wide-eyed, like an owl. I have lost my power of speech.

Perti looks hard at me. "Will you do as I say and go home immediately?"

I nod and, drawing strength I don't know where from, start walking. After a few steps I remember what Perti told me this morning: *I didn't know the guy they killed yesterday, and I don't care about what he was or what he did.* I look back. Perti has crossed the road already and is walking toward the church, with a firmer step than usual. I'm shocked; I can't believe that anticlerical Perti, skeptical Perti, blasphemous Perti, is actually going to a funeral. He opens the church door. I hear what must be the priest's voice, monotonous and without feeling, singing. Perti walks into the church and when he closes the door the singing is no longer audible. Just then, I hear loud, angry shouts and shrieks from the streets. The port is too far away, and anyway, it's too early for the festival to have started. Besides, the racket is getting louder and louder and doesn't sound at all like a party. It doesn't seem like a lot of people, but they are shouting as loudly as they can. The two policemen on the street corner and the other two by the garden start running toward the shouts. The photographer suddenly materializes and sprints after them.

"Psst!" I say to him as he passes me by. He turns and raises his eyebrows and shrugs his shoulders as if to ask what I want. He hasn't recognized me.

It occurs to me that I could take out a cigarette and ask him for a light.

But I turn my back on him, and without any more ado, leave the place; I couldn't care less if my shadow didn't follow.

24

I've read somewhere that sadness is not an infectious disease. At its worst, it pushes people away from you.

I enter the poplar-lined avenue hoping I'll be able to shake my sadness away. I shuffle through the fallen leaves and it seems to me they echo my downheartedness.

I reach our house and look up at the window. There's someone behind the net curtains. *Mom is waiting for me*, I think. I greet her with a nod. I think she has stepped back.

Life is returning to its usual pace, becoming routine; one day follows another along this path that leads us inexorably to death. One day.

Twenty-four hours have passed since I witnessed an assassination. Those images—the man looking at me as he died, the rivulets of blood, the purple flowers—are starting to blur, to blend in with the clouds, like ships disappearing in a sudden sea mist.

And it only happened yesterday, yesterday evening.

I sniff the air as I am about to cross the doorway.

The wind carries the moist smell of freshly dug earth.